THE DOCT

When Staff-Nurse Anna Forster meets the new
Senior Surgical Registrar at the Calderbury Royal
she realises that most clouds *do* have a silver lining.
It is love at first sight for Anna, but is it the same
for Paul Keslar?

*Books you will enjoy
in our Doctor—Nurse series*

THE DOCTOR'S DECISION

BY

ELIZABETH PETTY

MILLS & BOON LIMITED
London . Sydney . Toronto

First published in Great Britain 1981
by Mills & Boon Limited, 15–16 Brook's Mews,
London W1A 1DR

Australian copyright 1981
Philippine copyright 1981

ISBN 0 263 73716 0

Set in Monophoto Baskerville 11 on 11½ pt.

*Made and printed in Great Britain by
Richard Clay (The Chaucer Press, Ltd,
Bungay, Suffolk*

CHAPTER ONE

It was the kind of May morning which makes one want to burst into song for the sheer joy of being alive, Anna Forster decided, and the next moment she was competing with the lark winging up there under the cloudless blue sky, as she drove her small car along the winding lane on her way to the hospital.

The scent of apple blossom came in through the open window from orchards on either side; trees covered with clouds of tiny pink and white ballerinas against a blue backcloth, all so perfect. What a pity that in the first rain they would scatter into a white carpet beneath the trees. She had come to love this corner of Kent, in such contrast to the teaching hospital in London where she had been for four work-filled, drama-packed years.

She had missed it all at first; her friends, doctors and staff with whom she had been extremely popular, but she hadn't hesitated when a problem arose at home, and she had solved it by transferring to Calderbury Royal. So far she hadn't regretted it, loving the surrounding countryside.

Now she lived at home. In the high, round oast house which her father, a well-known geologist, had converted into a lovely home. He had also built in a tiny flat for his mother. When he had been asked to go to Iceland on a very special project, lasting two years, he quite naturally wanted Eve, his wife, to go too. But Gran couldn't be left alone although she insisted that she certainly didn't mind her own company.

So Anna had made the change, and although she found the hospital at Calderbury smaller and not so modern, she had fitted in well and went on enjoying what she was doing. Now—glancing at the watch pinned on her print dress—she saw that she was in good time. It was only four miles into the town centre. She particularly wanted to be early this morning because Mr Lonsdale's new senior registrar would be taking surgical outpatients with him for the first time. Anna hadn't met him yet, but she had caught his back view on Friday as she was coming down the stairs to start her weekend off-duty. She had noticed the steady, determined strides of the new registrar as he emerged from the Day Theatre with Mr Lonsdale and turned towards the wards.

Taller than the consultant, his dark head bent a little forward in a listening position, she saw that his thick hair was well shaped into his neck, though a little tousled from yanking off his theatre cap. Somehow, it made him seem vulnerable, which gave this particular Monday morning an air of curiosity, even excitement. She was looking forward to working with him and, as senior staff nurse, she could simplify his first day considerably; in fact he would expect her to do so.

She had to swerve just before the next blind corner as a landrover swung round it, and she caught a glimpse of Mervyn Abbot's fair hair and red-checked shirt. He and his brothers, with their father, farmed the land for miles around and lived a mile down the lane from the Oast House. On Saturday she had been invited to the May-Day Country and Western, in their barn, decorated for the occasion, and she smiled as she remembered what a hilarious affair it had turned out to be. The Abbot boys were mainly responsible for that.

Turning on to the main road, she saw that a traffic queue had already formed and lights were in operation. Why must they start road repairs on a Monday morning, she wondered, her usually smooth brow creasing into a frown when it seemed an age before the red light changed to green and she could move forward, only to change back again before she reached it. She sat niggled with impatience, her lighthearted mood gone. Thank goodness that Jill Slade, also a senior nurse, would be in to get things moving, and Nurse Grant was a good, reliable second-year student, so with luck she would soon catch up. Hopefully, Sister Dunn would be too preoccupied with the gynaecologist's clinic, at the other end of the hall, this morning; she knew she could trust surgical to look after itself.

She breathed with relief as the roundabout on the edge of town came into sight, moving to the inner lane and only just noticing Jill in the bus queue, frantically signalling to her to stop, and not in the treatment room at the Royal at all.

The other nurse slid thankfully into the seat beside Anna, looking anxious and frustrated as she burst out:

'Am I glad to see you, Staff? Do you know, I've been standing there for half an hour and no sign of a bus. I tried to thumb a lift but no-one was biting. We're late, aren't we?'

Anna nodded resignedly. ''Fraid so, Slade. I'll have to allow for delays like this tomorrow. I do hate starting a day this way. It was all so lovely to begin with. Barring hold-ups, we just might make it. How was your weekend? You were up on Regis, weren't you?'

Jill nodded. 'Not too bad. A bit hectic on Saturday afternoon. Mr Burton had a cardiac . . .'

'Oh, lord—who got it?'

'I did. You know how it is; the ward full of visitors—Sister off. Dr Keslar was soon there and the team. He made it—they've got him in Intensive still. How did yours work out? Did you go to the dance in the village?'

'Yes. It was good . . .'

'The Abbot lads were there, of course . . .'

'Everyone for miles around too, I should think.'

'Did Mervyn take you home, or shouldn't I ask?'

'He did. Along with a truck full of others to drop off in outlying cottages. I think everyone had too much home-made wine. It's lethal. But it was great fun and I enjoyed it. I was first out of the scrum, by request, getting myself dropped off at the gate.'

'Oh—I bet that wasn't Mervyn's intention.'

'He didn't seem to mind. They're a very chivalrous lot down there at the farm.'

'But wouldn't you have liked to be last? Just give *me* the chance . . .'

'It was late and Gran was on her own,' Anna said quickly, determined not to get in any deeper. Her feelings for Mervyn were at a rather transient stage, but he was becoming more than just interested in her. She felt that at any moment the interest could blow up into something more serious, on his side especially, and in such a tight community it could become awkward. Unless she too wanted to become involved. Just now, she was treading warily, but it was an exciting idea, just the same. Saturday night had developed into something she hadn't expected, with them dancing together most of the time, except in the more communal square dancing. The music, the heat, the wine and the lanterns had produced an unreal effect.

There had been an intensity about the way Mervyn had looked at her from his devastatingly blue eyes, then laughing down at her the next moment, drawing her as close as he dare, sending her composure crumbling. She had really let herself go—and she had really enjoyed herself after that.

Now her concentration on the heavy traffic heading for the main London route drove all other thoughts from her mind until they turned off, and the car sped up the hill towards the grey stone hospital at the top. Jill began to gather her things together and as they went in through the iron gates, remarked grimly,

'Just ten minutes, Staff. Oh—there's a parking space . . .'

Both girls literally ran towards the nurses' entrance, hoping they wouldn't run into anyone who mattered, but once in the changing room, the hospital atmosphere took over and Anna pinned on her clean, diminutive white cap without speaking. Her hair would have to do; she had already pinned it back in the twist she wore under her cap. First out of the door, with Jill right behind, they turned towards outpatients, stepping aside to let two porters through with a patient on a trolley, bound for X-ray. Outside, an ambulance klaxon sounded as it tore up to the Casualty entrance. Two minutes—if they were to arrive before the doctors—and there was still a long corridor to traverse before the waiting hall.

Anna groaned. 'Hope they're both late as well. Just a chance, I suppose, if they get stuck in the traffic too. Wonder where Dr Keslar comes from?'

'Haven't a clue.'

'I just hope Grant has got organised and that we don't meet Sister Dunn any minute now. She's on too, this morning,' Anna said, as they hurried past the Day Theatre and a row of trolleys waiting for patients. A group of students had arrived and stood waiting to be taken around the wards.

'Staff . . .' Jill said faintly, as they turned into the waiting hall where Mr Lonsdale and Dr Keslar's names appeared on the board, 'I've just re-membered, they've given us Willis. Grant's gone down with tonsilitis . . .'

'Oh—heavens. Poor kid . . .'

Patients were already filling the rows of blue plas-tic chairs, prepared for a long wait, yet they still came early. It was quite pleasant, with plenty of magazines and a fish tank, and white net curtains billowing in the breeze from an open window. Gone now the hard seats and white cold tiles on walls and floors of the past.

Anna's ready smile acknowledged one or two patients whom she knew, before turning into the smaller corridor with the consultant and treatment rooms opening from either side.

Her observant eyes noticed that Nurse Willis hadn't let her down as she apologised for their late arrival.

'We had traffic delays,' she explained, 'but you were certainly in early to have done all this. Thank you. Gosh—you've even got the reports in order with the list. Fortunately, Dr Keslar isn't here yet. He'll probably come in with Mr Lonsdale this morning.' She considered for a moment. 'Jill—I'll stick with Dr Keslar, I think, if you'll look after Mr Lonsdale, and Nurse Willis, I'm afraid you'll need to be where you're wanted at any given time. Keep your eyes open, won't you? It's good experience working on a clinic like this where most of the patients are post-operative or being seen by the surgeon for the first time. Do we need more dressings? Yes—the 10 × 10 Melamin are getting low, and Micropore—bandages seem all right. Oh—more gauze, please. I'll give you a list . . .'.

She ran her eyes over the instruments laid ready and receivers; in fact, everything needed for that day's clinic.

Jill, checking the other treatment room, reported that the folders were all on Mr Lonsdale's desk and everything looked fine.

'Can we go through these X-ray plates then, and check them with the folders?' Anna asked. 'Oh—we have a couple of cancellations too . . .'

Nurse Willis, arriving with the new supplies, got a special smile. Both nurses were relaxed now that the tensions from being late had passed. Anna's smile was normally spontaneous, coming from a naturally happy disposition, and she also had an imborn sensitivity for other people's feelings. Two things made her angry: injustice—either towards herself or others, and incompetence. Slap-dash work, she called it. She would let nothing slide and set her own standards. She had already promised herself that in no way would she be late again for duty. But it seemed that the two doctors, already ten minutes late, had fallen down too.

Her purple belt accentuated the small waist as she leaned over the table writing in a few notes of her own. Above her head in the darkened corridor, a light shone down on to pale gold hair, shiningly healthy. A tiny flaxen curl had escaped on to her

slender neck, feminine, and it was the first thing Paul
Keslar noticed when he and his Chief turned the
corner; but she didn't know this until much later.

Mr Lonsdale was looking pleased with himself this
morning. It was possible that his new registrar might
have something to do with that. Some of the pressures were off. He came up to Anna.

'Morning, Staff. Have you met Dr Keslar?'

Paul Keslar was already assessing her, forming his
own impressions, with wide apart, brownish eyes, she
thought, or were they a kind of golden hazel?
Difficult, in that brief moment, to be sure, before she
answered lightly that she had not. Then, as she introduced the rest of the staff, he asked,

'No Sister in charge?'

'Sister Dunn is overall Sister of the whole
Outpatients unit this morning, Dr Keslar.'

'I see.' It was his only remark before turning and
following the surgeon into his room. Anna's conjec-
ture was that nothing had escaped his eyes and that
he was very much on the ball. A man with very
definite inner resources who knew where he was
going and probably when he would arrive. She
wasn't as relaxed as usual when she went into the
consulting room a few seconds later. She hoped this
was only temporary because it was important that
there should be a good working relationship between
nursing staff and doctors, although, on duty, there
was always the dividing line, only crossed when off-
duty or at dances or parties, or sometimes behind
kitchen doors if two people had something special
going.

Now she stood waiting while Mr Lonsdale glanced
through the pile of folders on his desk and ran his
eye down the long list.

'I'll see the new patients, of course . . .' he included Anna as well as Dr Keslar; 'you, Paul, had better take this lot. See how you go. I'm here if you want me, but I can't see that happening. Admissions are a bit difficult because Thursday's list will take up the two empty beds they have on Rowan, but we usually get round it if it becomes essential.' He smiled up at Anna. 'I'll lend you my favourite Staff Nurse for today . . .'

But Paul Keslar, thoughtfully reading through some of the notes, didn't look up at once. When he did, he said briefly, 'I'd better get started then, Sir. We're late enough as it is.' Then noticing that Anna was holding open the door for him, he walked purposefully through into the corridor and stood waiting.

'In here, Dr Keslar,' she said. 'We use both treatment rooms . . .' she indicated the two doors leading from it. 'Mr Lonsdale also has another two adjoining his.'

'I see. A kind of shuttle service.'

'No. Just that patients can be seen more quickly if their dressings are removed while you are talking to the next one—it does save time.'

'Staff Nurse—Forster, wasn't it? You are not instructing a student, you know. I have come from a top London hospital, four times the size of this one, and from what I have seen so far, much more efficiently run. And what I do not need this morning is a Staff Nurse fussing like a mother hen. Now—shall we get on? I'll see my first patient, please.'

The prickle of rising anger was soon quelled. Anna, taken by surprise, would think about it later. She had only been trying to help. Her voice was quietly controlled when she asked, 'Which patient would you like in first, Dr Keslar?'

He was absorbed in the notes in his hand, looking up with raised eyebrows, his eyes unwavering as they met hers.

'Mrs Thorpe, of course. She is on top here . . .'

'Oh, dear,' Anna groaned inwardly as she went to call in the patient. Was this a foretaste of what it would be like working with the new registrar, or had something upset him this morning?

After that, she was careful not to volunteer any information which might have helped him further, standing quietly in the background concentrating on his needs or those of the patient. But neither did he seem to expect any help. He worked without fuss, confidently, greeting each patient as if they were the only one being seen that day. Each time he introduced himself.

'I'm Dr Keslar—Mr Lonsdale's registrar. Now— tell me—how have you been since we last saw you?' And really listening to their answers.

So the morning moved along and Anna worked beside him, sending patients away with their wounds redressed and making sure they understood the instructions given for treatment at home, or when to come again. Or standing beside Dr Keslar, anticipating his request for instruments or dressings, listening while he made his decisions, firmly and without hesitation, and now she found her respect for him growing hourly.

Only twice did he cross the corridor to consult with his senior, about a need for further surgery in both cases.

Later, returning from a short coffee break, Anna saw that the chairs in the waiting area were still fully occupied and resigned herself to a longer morning session than usual. Lunch would be a quick snack for both doctors. When she went into the small treatment room, Dr Keslar, examining a post-operative incision, stretched out an arm without looking round.

'Stitch cutters, Nurse.'

Willis, hovering by the door, hesitated just long enough for Anna to get them. She signalled for the nurse to go for her coffee break and asked quietly, 'Would you like me to take them out, Dr Keslar?'

He straightened up and looked down at her under half-closed lids.

'Please. I didn't know you were back.'

Suddenly, she was close to him, mentally and physically, because, as he leaned over to examine his patient's thigh with its recent skin graft, his white coat touched her bare arm and she smelled his cologne, sharp and clean, and something happened to her throat. She swallowed hard, willing her hands to be controlled and cool again. But there was no doubt that his nearness had affected her strangely. It also seemed to be getting hotter in the room. He must have felt it too, because he went to open two more windows himself before coming back to watch as each discoloured suture was deposited from the tweezers on to a piece of gauze. So far the patient hadn't made a sound.

'You're being very brave,' Anna said quietly, 'these last two are a bit messy though. I'll try not to hurt you more than I have to. Hold tight.'

It was Paul Keslar who put his firm hand over the woman's trembling one and held her leg still. As he talked to his patient, Anna stood silently waiting, her first opinion of him changed completely.

'It still feels very sore, does it?' he asked.

'Oh, yes,' the woman said faintly. 'It looks dreadful, doesn't it? I'll never be able to wear a swim suit again, will I?'

'Well—does it really matter? In time it won't notice too much. I know you won't believe this, but to me it looks beautiful. It's a perfect graft and you are going to be fine. Just give it time. I'm quite sure your husband would rather have you as you are, than as might have happened if this hadn't been detected, with far worse problems we couldn't have coped with. Why don't you try asking him?'

'He says the same thing, Doctor.'

'Well, then. Concentrate on getting mobile and I'll see you again in two weeks. Goodbye.'

As he went towards the door he said crisply, 'Melamin dressings over sofra tulle, Staff Nurse.'

As if I didn't know, Anna thought, as she tore open the dressings and applied them carefully. There was no time to day-dream, but she would have liked to. Her patient also seemed to have been captivated, relieved now that her ordeal was over.

'He's nice, isn't he?' she confided. 'What a splendid doctor.'

'Yes. He is nice,' Anna agreed. 'Very . . .'

The next patient was already in with him. She heard his chair scrape on the floor as he rose to close the door.

As she had anticipated, it was a long day and not every case was straightforward. The writing part alone was enough to exhaust most doctors, apart from the decision-making, responsibility and patient assessment needed every minute. A surgical clinic is different from any other and a surgical registrar can afford no let ups, even if he is protected by his surgeon.

It was almost five o'clock when Mr Lonsdale came over into Paul Keslar's room, without his white coat.

'God—I'm whacked,' he said, as he sat down opposite the table. 'Are you through, Paul?'

'Yes, Sir. Just.' He waited as Anna took his completed notes.

'How did it go? Find it wearying?'

'As I expected, Sir. Varied and interesting. Is it always this busy?'

Mr Lonsdale nodded. 'Almost always, isn't it, Staff?' He smiled up at Anna, gathering up the rest of the folders.

'Yes. I'm afraid so.' She relaxed into one of her spontaneous smiles, encountering Dr Keslar's raised eyebrows and concentrated glance as he massaged the back of his neck.

The colour rushed to her face as she went out quickly; it was even worse when she overheard Paul Keslar say sceptically, 'Good heavens—I didn't know girls blushed any more.'

'Perhaps,' Dr Lonsdale murmured, 'you've been cultivating the wrong girls, Paul. Some of our nurses are extremely decorative, as well as being efficient, as you must have noticed already. It makes the day more pleasurable, don't you think? Now—I'd like your observations on a new patient I admitted today, so shall we go up to Rowan Ward?'

The two men emerged. Anna and the other nurses were checking dressings and clearing up. In answer to the surgeon's 'Goodnight, Staff . . .' she said quietly, still with the smile which was a natural part of her image, 'Goodnight, Sir.'

But it was noticeable that Paul Keslar didn't say anything as the two men's shoes hit the floor rythmically until they turned the corner on their way up to Rowan Ward, a mixed surgical where patients underwent surgery and were then filtered into Regis before being sent out.

She liked working on Rowan, even though it was tough going. She could imagine both doctors there now, going from bed to bed as Mr Lonsdale checked on his own list. She had almost been on the point of asking to be transferred back there herself, but now, she wasn't so sure. A new and unspoken challenge seemed to have arisen down here in outpatients, crying out to be met first. Today was only the beginning, she was already looking forward to tomorrow. It was even an exhilarating thought and, coming at the end of a busy Monday, a bit out of context.

'I think that's it,' Jill broke into her thoughts as she stood on tiptoe to push a box on to the top of a cupboard turning to survey Anna. 'Well?' she asked, with her head on one side. 'What about our new registrar, then? A bit "keep off the grass", isn't he?'

Anna, quick to defend him, said softly, 'He's got a sensitive approach to the patients though, and he's marvellous to work with. You know exactly where you are with him . . .'

'Really? Well—after Dr Cannon . . . He was so ambitious, it wasn't true. But you have to admit, he was dynamic.'

'Patients with very sore wounds don't usually want that kind of dynamism and heavy prodding,' Anna said slowly. 'Dr Keslar is gentle, but I'm quite sure he could be just as dynamic—in the right place.'

'And the right time,' Jill giggled. 'Wonder if he's married?'

'I haven't a clue,' Anna said sharply, for her. 'It's time we weren't here, anyway. I'm off.'

'Hang on. I'm coming. Can you give me a lift to the bus station?'

'Of course. What about you, Nurse Willis?'

'I'm living in the hostel.'

'Oh, yes. Okay then. See you tomorrow. Goodnight.'

It was still bright and sunny as the two girls left the hospital building and walked over to the parked car. Anna put her face up, feeling the breeze through her loosened hair like soft fingers, unaware that Paul Keslar, standing by the ward window while Mr Lonsdale was having a talk with Sister, was looking down at her, his expression inscrutable as he watched the small cream car move out through the gates before he turned back to the row of beds behind him.

Anna, relaxed now, felt an enormous lifting of her spirit, and, after dropping Jill at the bus station, felt her tiredness disappearing, leaving only relief and pleasure as she drove back through the lanes to the Oast House. Overhead, trees overhung, their branches casting golden shadows on the road. She couldn't explain her feeling that life seemed suddenly so full of promise, with so much to look forward to, and her new exhilaration stemming from just one moment in the surgery that morning. A little thrust of excitement shot through her and a smile trembled on her lips as she remembered.

Turning in through the gates, she saw her grandmother waiting for her.

At seventy, Jane Forster was still a healthy-looking lady. Her white hair shone in the evening sun and the blue knitted suit looked good on her elegant figure as she came to meet her grand-daughter.

'Hullo, Gran. Had a nice day?'

'Lovely, dear. How was yours?'

'Hectic.' They walked towards the house and then Anna said, as if she could no longer keep the news to herself,

'Did I tell you that we were having a new registrar?'

Jane nodded; she also caught the inflection in Anna's voice. 'You did. And what is he like? Do you get on with him?'

'Oh—of course. He's not very outgoing—I mean, it would be difficult to get to know him well, as a person, unless he wanted you to.'

'Good-looking? Tall, lean, short or fat?'

'Oh—Gran. You're teasing again. Not exactly good-looking; but he has got rather nice eyes and quite a strong face. He doesn't wrap things up— I mean, he can be abrupt, but he's sensitive to patients and very good at his job . . .' she finished slowly.

'Quite a summary. Is he married?'

'I—don't know.' She stood up abruptly. 'I'll just go up and change and take Shane for his walk. Is there time before supper? It smells good, Gran. What is it?'

'Just casseroled beef, dear. With a little of your father's red wine . . .'

'You'll get shot,' Anna grinned. 'Only two more weeks and they'll be home on holiday. It will be nice to see them.'

'Yes. It was Christmas when they were here last. I can't imagine Christmas being the same in Iceland somehow. Not the atmosphere as we know it. A bit austere, wouldn't you think? But then, they are a people who live simply and are very down to earth. Enterprising too; I think I'd like to visit there some-day.'

'Perhaps you will. The climate is good during the summer months. I was reading somewhere the other day that they have an extremely low death rate and are long-lived. It makes you think, doesn't it, that they could teach us a thing or two with their simple diet and life style.'

'I'm sure of it. Supper in half an hour, then.'

'Right. I'll get changed.'

A few minutes later, wearing comfortable shoes and slacks, Anna turned off the lane into the woods, feeling the soft brown leafmould beneath her feet. Every shade of green surrounded her as she stood still and let the quiet and peace seep into her.

There were bluebells now as far as she could see, and, as she went further in, they became interspersed with the taller, wild pink campions and even taller thistles, their purple clusters of flowers just opening. She caught her breath at the perfect combination of colour; nature's own exhibition in this natural set-ting. She desperately wanted to share it with someone. It was almost too perfect in the stillness, a sight to be treasured. But without any warning, in sharp contrast, the bigger part of her life came into focus—the hospital and all the stark reality of pain and surgical emergencies and people—drama within the wards and theatres; immediate decisions of the surgeons and specialists dedicated to saving lives, and she felt subdued at once.

Anna had decided to become a nurse while still at school. It was after seeing the care given to her grandfather whom she had loved dearly, spending a lot of time at his hospital bed while he was ill. Her observant eyes had taken heed of the dependence a patient felt towards the nursing staff and the acute shortage of nurses even then, as one of the nurses remarked when she adjusted his saline drip: 'What we really need is at least another pair of hands on the ward.' She had seen the Sister in charge doing tasks which should have been done by others. She knew then what she wanted to do with her own future and set about getting the necessary qualifications for training. Now—it was her own profession. Not once had it even occurred to her to change direction, even after four incredibly hard years. And still the old maxim prevailed, 'Oh—for another pair of hands.'

She called to Shane, half-way down a fox hole under a withered elm, and when he came obediently, his nose covered in sandy earth, she fastened the chain to his collar before stepping out into the lane.

The landrover, with Mervyn driving, appeared from nowhere, stopped, and he stuck his tousled head from the window, grinning down at Anna, waiting for her to look as pleased to see him as he obviously was to see her.

'Hullo, there . . .' His teeth white in an already tanned face, grubby with the sweat and soil of a day's work begun very early, and not over yet.

'Hullo, Mervyn. Still at it?' She had to look at him although he disconcerted her.

'Almost through now. Why don't you come down to the Plough tonight? There's a match on . . .'

She shook her head. 'Thanks all the same. I really have things I must do.'

'Saturday, then. You're coming to the barbecue aren't you? It'll be fun.'

'Well—I'm on duty until seven-thirty doing a

stand-in on the wards this weekend. Maybe later.'

'I want you to come, Anna. Can I come up for you?'

'No—I'll drive down if I'm not out on my feet,' she said, well aware that his eyes were trying to tell her something.

He shook his head. 'I just don't get it. How on earth do they still manage to recruit nurses when they have to work such unholy hours?'

She shrugged. 'We get used to it and we know it all when we go into it—besides, you're still working.'

'Ah—but it's for ourselves and is only seasonal. I really mean it when I say it won't be the same if you aren't there on Saturday.'

She could no longer ignore the expression in his blazingly blue eyes, alight with mischief, and he meant that she shouldn't.

She shook her head laughingly and promised, 'Saturday, then.'

His arm, the sleeve rolled up above the elbow, was still waving as he drove on down to the farm. Her lips were still curved into a smile as she stood looking after him. Life and work were all fun to him.

Saturday's hilarity would mean another effort by the village community for miles around to keep something special alive in the countryside, and she would go along with it. Besides, she was young enough and woman enough to appreciate that Mervyn was definitely attracted towards her, and she had to admit that she too had enjoyed the strength of his arms around her, while the band had throbbed its way through the evening. And she needed some escapism, apart from her books and records and tight social life because of the unsocial hours she kept.

But, she asked herself, as she went across the lawn to the tall, round house; escape from what? The hospital? Pressures? Patients? Why, when she loved what she was doing? Nursing was what she found most fulfilling.

She bent to let Shane go free and, quite without warning, Paul Keslar's face came into focus in her mind. His eyes, clearly defined now, thoughtful and expressive, more serious, more stressful than the rougish face of Mervyn whom she had so recently left. Two men, not remotely alike, yet both part of her thoughts tonight.

She was a little unsure of the way those thoughts were going as she went into the house, nor why she was breaking a firm rule, twice in one evening, which was never to bring the hospital in any form home with her, never to get involved with patients or the hospital staff. It had been fairly easy to leave it behind and keep her life in separate parts; one had to—until now.

CHAPTER TWO

A SOFT rain was falling next morning when Anna walked across the grass to her car. She had wakened to a feeling of restlessness for which there was no apparent reason. On impulse she lifted her face to feel the drenching fresh touch of rain and found it immediately soothing to her skin and also her mood.

Today, she encountered fewer of the difficulties experienced yesterday, because she was that much earlier probably, and arrived in good time in the car park at the hospital. Changing her shoes and donning her cap took only a few minutes and by the time she was ready for duty her usually calm approach to the day ahead had asserted itself.

Dr Keslar was also ahead of time this morning as he came striding along the corridor in his white coat, having already been to see a patient on Rowan. Recognising the assured walk and slim, belted waist of the nurse in front, he quickened his pace a little, noticing the way she held her head—and what hair!—like corn silk; though why that expression came directly to mind he couldn't imagine. It amused him, because although he was no more immune to female charms than the next man, he had so far drawn the line at the nursing staff in his own hospital; well, since his early student days anyway; but this girl was different. Warning lights were already flashing, which was enough to bring on his more taciturn approach, which Anna soon noticed and found inexplicable as he swished past her, white coat flying and with a curt, 'Good morning' went straight into his room.

There was activity outside in the waiting hall as the first patients began to register in and Nurse Willis was sent to collect the X-ray envelopes which hadn't yet been delivered. Jill was busy in the other two treatment rooms while Anna checked the rather formidable pile of folders with her own list.

When she went in to Dr Keslar he was standing with his back to the room watching the steady downpour outside as cars splashed into the empty spaces, but he turned at once. Anna met his speculative gaze for a brief second only, before he held out his hand for the folders and, pulling his chair forward with one foot, sat down facing her.

'Are these all of them?'

'No. I've left Mr Lonsdale's on his desk.'

'He's going to be late, did you know?'

'Well—he likes to go up to the wards first on Tuesdays, so he often doesn't get down here until around ten.'

'I see.' He glanced at his watch. 'I'd better get started then. Mr Handly first, please.'

She sent Nurse Willis to bring in the patient, standing back while he was verbally quizzed, before Paul Keslar glanced up.

'I'll examine Mr Handly, Nurse, if you'll get him ready. In there, please.'

Something was disturbing him this morning. Anna sensed it at once, though it was under control. She resented slightly the cool note in his voice when he addressed her. What on earth could she have done wrong? She felt her resistance ebbing a little under the strength of his personality. If Nurse Slade thought he wasn't dynamic then she was in for a surprise sometime. Every movement seemed to be calculated and determined today. He had a way with him, usually not achieved until consultant level, which was where he was heading, obviously.

Two patients were admitted during the first hour as emergencies. One, an older woman, already attending Mr Lonsdale's clinic for persistent abdominal pain, had developed an acute strangulated hernia in the early hours of that morning and was determined to keep her appointment. She needed immediate surgery and was wheeled, together with an anxious husband, up to Rowan Ward.

The other patient was young and actually collapsed in Dr Keslar's consulting room as he was being questioned. As he was a new patient, there were a lot of details about him to be written down in his report. Age, twenty-two; not married; almost forced to come to the hospital and then only by remittent pain, and referred by his G.P.

'Why have you put up with it this long?' Dr Keslar asked, looking up from his notes.

'Can't bear the thought of an operation,' he shrugged. 'Usually it goes after a time—but . . .'

'This is worse . . .?'

'Yes. I . . . Oh . . .' He leaned sideways, his hands pressed to his abdomen. He was sweating profusely and the same thought occurred to Anna and to the registrar at the same moment. Their eyes met in the awareness of a sudden emergency.

'Can you walk, Mr Young? I'd like to have a look at you.' He put his hand under the sick man's elbow to help him off the chair. Anna was already there on his other side. 'You know this appendix must come out right now, don't you?'

The patient had passed out.

'Perforated?' Anna said quickly as Paul Keslar picked up the phone.

'I'm afraid so.' She supported the unconscious man while he spoke to the senior surgical officer and the wheels were set in motion for yet another emergency operation. Theatre staff would be alerted, providing there was a free theatre not already in use and, if so, it would be fitted in between other more routine ops today. Students were being used as dressers at the moment which would help out the staff shortage and already the trolley wheels were sounding in the corridor and Dr Keslar opened the door for them.

Anna took his folder and went out to Nurse Willis. 'Go along with Mr Young, Nurse,' she said, 'and stay with him until you are told to return. Here are his notes.'

Mr Lonsdale raised his eyebrows as he came down the corridor.

'Good morning, Staff. Problems?'

'It's all right now, Sir. Dr Keslar saw him before he collapsed.'

He went on into his room, making no further comment, but a moment later he again opened his door.

'Will you ask Dr Keslar to come in here when he has finished with his patient, Staff Nurse?'

'Yes, Sir.'

Paul Keslar didn't comment when she passed on the request but there was a set look about his chin which confirmed her intuitive feeling that something was not quite right somewhere and disturbed him this morning. She was also starting a headache, due, no doubt, to the oppressiveness outside. It was better when it was actually raining. The thunder had decided to correlate around the area hemmed in and lightning was streaking across the sky vividly every few minutes and was disturbing.

After lunch, Anna began to feel almost protective towards the registrar as he faced yet another patient across his table, noticing so much in that first appraisal as he said, 'Hullo. Do sit down. Well—how are you?'

Everywhere there was a smell of damp clothes, raincoats and over-warm bodies. The pressure seemed heavier than ever and Anna's head was positively throbbing when she slipped out to ask Nurse Willis to go into the room and help the patient, a woman, to undress ready for Dr Keslar to examine her. She took two tablets and swallowed some water and ran the cold tap over her wrists before returning, surprised to see his white-coated figure emerge from the treatment room. She wasn't prepared for the cold anger in his voice. Nurse Willis was nowhere in sight and she guessed what had happened immediately. Mr Lonsdale had also called her into his room.

'Is it asking too much, Staff Nurse, for my patients to be ready for me? Or am I expected to remove their dressings myself as well?'

She kept a cool approach, passing him before she said quietly, 'I am sorry . . .' and closing the door. But he was already undoing the bandage, dropping it into the soiled dressings bin and washing his hands while looking back at her over his shoulder.

'I do need those removed also,' he said crisply. 'Is something wrong, Nurse?'

'No, Dr Keslar. I have the tweezers ready.' To her horror her fingers were trembling. He took them from her and gently lifted the soaked layers of tulle,

dropping them into the receiver she now held. She
hoped she wasn't sickening for something, a chill or
worse, because now her hands were icy cold in com-
parison with a burning forehead.

'I'll take these out too, I think,' he said, almost to
himself. 'Stitch cutters . . .'

She could imagine him in the theatre now and
hoped she would work with him there sometime.
Turning to respond to his request, she picked them
up then, unbelievably, she felt them slide on to the
floor, her fingers not even grasping properly. She
felt nauseated as she bent to pick them up, closing
her eyes not to see the sharp look he gave her.

'I'll have some more brought from the sterilizer.'

'Surely there is another one . . .'

She shook her head. 'No. I'm sorry.'

'Then there should be. See that there are in future,
please.'

There was perspiration on his forehead too. In the
theatre she would have mopped it away but he
seemed unapproachable. Yet he turned to speak to
his patient and his voice was suddenly gentle.

Anna began to collect fresh dressings from the
table. At least she would have those ready.

What on earth could be wrong with her? It was
true, thunder often did upset her physically, but
there was more to it than that. Today had been extremely busy with a lot of to and froing; and, to save
him, forms and path lab reports and patients sent for
blood tests, all needing a cool head, which was what
she hadn't got today, so the concentration was even
greater. She shouldn't be feeling the strain, but she
was, simply because there was only one student nurse
between them. Probably Nurse Slade was feeling the
same way. They had only had vague glimpses of

each other as they whisked in and out of the doors.

She stood with the packets of Melolin in one hand and the tweezers in her other, waiting until he straightened up, deciding that Melolin wasn't enough yet.

'We'll bandage also . . .' he said curtly. Everything seemed slightly unreal as she took the correct size from the box. She felt herself sway against the chair and was about to turn and go to the bed with it when it too slid away from under her fingers, to roll across the damp floor, marked by wet shoes, coming to rest right in the corner. She watched it disbelievingly. 'Oh . . . no . . .'

Afterwards she wondered if her groan was audible, before bending to retrieve it and dropping it, with the other dressings, into the bin and starting back to take another one. He was beside her, his coat soft and smooth, his fingers cool on her wrist. She was surprised and looked up at him, willing some control to return.

Then, just as suddenly, his fingers were gone and his back was turned while she unwrapped a fresh bandage and started to apply it. This time, there were no slip-ups, and he was speaking quietly to his patient and the room was soon empty, Anna watching her go with some relief.

Through the open door she heard her name.

'Come in, Staff Nurse Forster, please.'

She went, expecting she knew not what; half angry with him as well as herself, and not ready to face him yet. His hand on her wrist had created yet another impact, her heart had reacted in no uncertain way, so that she could not ignore it.

'Sit down.'

'There are three more patients . . .'

'Sit down. You've been working like an automaton since eight-thirty this morning. Are you all right now?'

She nodded. 'I haven't done anything so stupid since my first year. I'm sorry . . .'

'Forget about that. I owe you an apology. It's probably overdue. By the way, Mr Lonsdale is demanding another nurse for tomorrow. This set-up is ridiculous.'

'We've been managing for quite a long time, Dr Keslar . . .'

'There seems to be an acute shortage of other things than nurses in this hospital but, whatever my reaction to these things, I shouldn't have taken it out on you. I'm sorry. Now, go for your tea break or whatever, because I warn you, we're having students in a few minutes for the rest of the afternoon; and I shall need you with me. Send me Nurse Willis and—don't be away long. I'll need you.'

She wasn't, because she wanted to be back with him again, refusing to admit to the very remote possibility that she could be falling in love with the new registrar. It only happened in the imaginations of romantic authors, never in the stark reality of day-to-day hospital routine. But she hadn't felt in the least attracted to any of the men she had worked with before, neither housemen nor registrars and certainly not any of the consultants. Admired them, yes, enjoyed the off-duty atmosphere and repartee at dances or parties, but to fall deeply in love? Well, that just was not on. So she would be on her guard in future and watch her rather feminine, tender thoughts towards Paul Keslar. Just because he had asked 'Are you all right?' in a caring voice which had meant she couldn't look at him immediately.

It was a relief to leave the hospital behind that evening. Her thoughts were still rather indeterminate, even though she was resolved to get things into a proper perspective before tomorrow. And then the Oast House came into view and she was driving through the gate. Putting the car away she didn't go into the house at once but stood looking out at the surrounding countryside. How lucky she was to have this to come home to. Four years in the nurses' hostel had made her appreciate that many nurses returned to a stuffy flat in the evenings, or not even that. This was sheer heaven. There were white clouds drifting across a blue sky, eased of its burden of thunderheads and angry streaks of electricity. Now the sun felt warm on her shoulders, but she decided to go in when the mosquitos began to settle on her hair, swarming from the damp warmth of the marshes.

Her grandmother was out somewhere and she picked up the letter from the mat bearing an Icelandic postmark and sat down to read it, refusing to be side-tracked by Shane's heavy paws, reminding her that he wanted to walk.

'You can't imagine how much we are looking forward to being home for a spell,' her mother had written. 'Especially just now. Are the bluebells out in the woods? Will they wait for us, do you think? Our flight is booked and we are longing to see you all . . .'

'Oh—me too,' Anna echoed, putting the letter back for her grandmother to read. Then, resolutely pulling on her rubber boots, she took Shane's chain off the hook and, locking the door, set off with him bounding beside her.

In the quiet of the woods her thoughts were

allowed to ramble too, because it was her private place. No need here to keep up the outward control for which she had been trained and which she had let slip today. Her face burned at the recollection. Why? It must never happen again. It was partly the atmospheric conditions and her work load, but, nevertheless . . . She stopped suddenly on the soft, squelching brown moss under her boots, her heart beats quickening because Paul Keslar's white-coated image and dark head with its questioning eyes was quite clear in her mind's eye and she was impatient to see him again, looking forward to tomorrow with an almost intense eagerness. How had she got so involved? In just two days. And how did she think she was going on working beside him if each time he was near her she behaved like a nervous teenager; which wasn't very funny either, as she well remembered from her own experience.

'So—Staff Nurse Forster,' she said aloud, 'you just pull yourself together from now on.' The determination in her voice made even Shane stop digging and look up at her.

An extra nurse arrived on outpatients next morning. For the first time Anna saw the hint of a smile when Dr Keslar came into the consulting room looking actually pleased to see her there too. She smiled back and called for the first patient. Their third day, and it was a lovely one and getting better all the time. She didn't mind how busy they were—and they were busy as they worked together non-stop.

Even Mr Lonsdale began to look pale and weary towards four o'clock. Dr Keslar went in to discuss an impending operation on tomorrow's list and she heard the surgeon say,

'Like to have a go at this one yourself, Paul?'

'Very much, Sir. I've only done one before.'

'Here's a chance for your second, then. Now—how are we going to fit Mr Leslie in?'

'I could get in and do him first, if you think it can be arranged . . .' Paul suggested.

'Have a word with Sister on Rowan, and Dr Lancing. Have you met her?'

'No. I think she's been away for a few days . . .'

'Of course. But she is back. I saw her this morning. Get them to have Mr Leslie pre-medicated early and in theatre by eight-thirty. Means an early morning for you . . .'

'I don't mind that, Sir. Quite looking forward to it . . .'

'Good heavens. Are you really?'

Anna, in the next room, wished that she could be in theatre next day, but it was Mr Lonsdale's operating day and her free one this week. She missed Rowan still, she had to admit wistfully.

Dr Keslar left before her and she guessed he was on his way up to the ward and his first meeting with Dr Lancing. He was in for a pleasant surprise because she was a very attractive girl, with dark hair almost to her shoulders and lovely brown eyes, and beneath the white coat which was never buttoned, even Anna conceded, was an extremely curvaceous figure. She was also extremely conscientious and hard-working. Those two would get on well together, especially as they were both comparative new-comers to the Royal. They'd have a lot in common. This thought gave her a definite lowering of her spirits as she finished clearing up for the day and sent the folders back to Records and noted Mr Lonsdale's written reports and queries. She was the last to leave, Jill and the student nurses having gone already.

She came out into the car park just in time to see Dr Keslar getting into a dark green Citroen. Certainly not the latest model, in fact, like her own, it was probably six years old at least.

She wondered where home was for him. A flat or even a house? Was he married? No, she was sure not. But he must have someone to look after him. His shirts, fresh each morning so far, looked immaculate. Now, wearing just a blue and white shirt and navy tie, he stretched one long, navy clad leg into his car and then the other and closed the door. He looked much more approachable now as, recognising her, he drove by. But he didn't smile at her. In fact, his expression was quite serious as their eyes clashed briefly.

'Oh, dear . . .' she thought philosophically, bending to turn her car key, 'we're back where we started. Square one, that is.' And because tomorrow was his theatre day she would be right outside that workload with its routine drama.

Thursday passed quickly. She worked in the garden and caught up with some reading, a large part of which consisted of written lectures by research tutors directed towards the nursing faculty.

Mervyn Abbot pulled up at the gate in the late afternoon, waiting for her to go and speak to him, which she had to do.

'Day off?' He was searching her eyes again.

'Yes.'

'If I'd known I could have arranged to finish early and take you somewhere.'

She shook her head laughingly, not wanting to appear rude. 'It's nice to be able to laze around here. I honestly don't feel like making the effort even to go into town, Mervyn.'

'Well—there's still Saturday. I'm looking forward to you being there—you know that, don't you, Anna?'

'Yes. I am too.'

Now why on earth had she said that? Well—in a way, she was, but he was going to misinterpret it. He already had.

'Good. Till Saturday then.'

She listened to his engine die away before she took her arms from the five-bar gate on which she had been leaning to talk to him; she felt a little disconcerted. But why? She had a date. So what?

Consulting her diary when she went into the house, she decided that she and Gran should do a bit of stocking up soon for her parents' return. Also, because the Whitsun holiday was approaching and that meant long queues at the supermarket.

'What about tomorrow evening, Gran? They stay open until eight and we don't have to go into town. The one on the Grange Road is good. I shouldn't be too late home tomorrow because Mr Lonsdale goes off at lunch time and I'll stand in for Sister on Rowan for the afternoon. Then I'm free. So shall we make out a list?'

Gran agreed, looking forward to having Anna around next evening. Then tentatively asking,

'Did I see you talking to one of the Abbot boys at the gate?'

'You know you did.'

'Going to the barbecue on Saturday with him?'

'Well—not actually with him. I'm on ward duty on Saturday which means I shan't be home until seven at the earliest.'

'What a pity.'

Anna didn't answer. Her thoughts were her own.

Mr Lonsdale saw only a limited number of patients on Fridays, alternating between them and his in-patients and private ones away from the hospital. Anna was on duty with him with Nurse Willis; Dr Keslar was not on call in outpatients at all that morning. She didn't see him until during the afternoon when she was relieving Sister on Rowan and he came into the ward with Dr Lancing. It was an unusual moment when Anna looked up and saw him for the first time on the ward where she felt more at home than anywhere in the hospital.

The two doctors walked slowly, in discussion about a patient probably, he with his eyes on the floor so that he didn't see Anna until they stopped at her table. By that time she had stilled the quick, exciting jab which had shot through her chest at sight of him.

'Oh—you're here, er—Nurse Forster . . .'

She wanted to say, 'Where did you expect me to be?' but she had been trained to stand quietly and wait, although she noticed that Dr Lancing gave her a quick look before going back to the folder in her hand.

'We'd like to see Mr Leslie, Staff—he's over here, isn't he? I wrote him up a B.P. chart. How's it been?' she asked in a soft voice.

'He's more stable now, Dr Lancing.'

If only she wasn't so physically aware of Paul Keslar. Heavens—this man's personality overwhelmed her every time. She followed his white coat tails to the patient's bed, standing back once she had placed the sheets for their examination. Because it was the first time she had seen him on the wards he took on a new image for her as he bent over the bed, his thinking directed only towards the patient's symptoms and condition. One could almost see his brain working as he asked questions and absorbed the answers.

When they had finished the two doctors went back to her table, conferring together and, after drawing back the curtains and asking gently, 'All right, Mr Leslie?', she went to join them, writing quickly on to the report the new medication ordered. When he made to go around the post-op patients in general, she again waited to go with him. But he shook his head.

'Dr Lancing and I can manage on our own, Staff Nurse. I'm sure you have other things to do.'

'Very well, Dr Keslar.' Her head was high and her shoulders well back as she went to find the nurse on duty with her. Visiting was from three until eight most days and already there were flowers lying around on the beds and a relative waiting to speak to her. Perhaps she could persuade Dr Keslar to do that—or Dr Lancing. It was, after all, one of their responsibilities.

A situation had arisen which was making her feel a little unlike her normal, happy self. In fact, she was conscious of a disgruntled niggle somewhere in her consciousness, running along her nerve ends so that she picked up some papers and put them down again on her return to the table. This was ridiculous. Maybe a quick cup of tea was indicated. Lunch had been scrappy—just a sandwich and glass of milk. She hoped they wouldn't expect one too. The clock on the ward wall gave her five minutes before she must check a couple of dressings and make sure she had carried out the other instructions Sister had left. Oh, yes—she had to make a phone call. One elderly patient was going to a convalescent home out of town and somehow the relatives must be contacted. She'd do that first.

Dr Keslar and the house doctor went past the kitchen door conversing together. She heard her light laugh at something he said. It didn't matter, of course, or it shouldn't—but the brightness seemed to have gone out of the day, making it just an ordinary routine one after all. It was her own fault, for thinking. But what had she imagined? Because of his cool hand on her wrist in an unprecedented moment of stress?

'Nurse . . .'

A desperate call from a very ill lady sent her feet going towards her bed, drawing the pale yellow and white curtains around it while she made her more comfortable. And from then on there was no time to think of anything but her work, as her feet traversed the long ward and she was immersed in the patients' needs or medication. But no-one grumbled too much on Rowan. Anna found it a satisfying ward because every patient was dependent on the nursing staff and there was an extremely caring Sister-in-charge for Rowan and Regis, and because she never spared herself, her nurses gave their last ounce as well. The male patients, once they were over the worst, were very vulnerable and a special relationship developed usually because of the nature of their operations. Both tact and privacy had to be ensured to make progress. Sometimes, there was some light bantering, because no two patients were alike, but it was all part of the therapy and anything which raised a giggle was only good for morale.

The patient next to Sister's table was groaning

and in some distress and Anna was glad, as she drew
his curtains, to see the navy dress of Sister going into
her office. She went to call her.

'Can you look at Mr Dennis, Sister? He's in some
pain . . .'

She glanced at her watch. 'I can't possibly give
him another injection yet, Staff. I'll come and have
a look at him. It's six o'clock, you know.'

'I'll stay and help with supper.'

'Are you sure? I'd be very grateful . . .'

The trolley wheels were already sounding along
the corridor and the smell of soup made for a general
movement among the patients.

Sister came back as Anna brought the trolley into
the ward and was asking the second-year nurse to
get the trays circulated around the beds.

'Will you get Dr Keslar bleeped, Staff?'

'Yes, Sister. Do you want me there?'

'No. Carry on if you will. It'll give the patients
something else to think about.' She hurried back
behind the curtains again, while Anna began the
task of filling soup dishes and going from bed to
bed, her eyes checking the list for special menus or
diets. Oh dear—for another pair of hands—she
thought quickly, barely looking up as Dr Keslar
and the house doctor came through the ward to
disappear behind the drawn curtains.

'Nurse . . .' a man's voice called, 'Mr Grange is
trying to sit up,' and she turned just in time to
prevent a drip being disconnected and more problems.

'I'll be back in a moment to give you your soup,
Mr Grange. Just be still . . .'

It was Sister who helped Dr Keslar wheel in the
oxygen trolley and Dr Lancing who stayed with him

while Dr Keslar wrote notes at the table once the emergency was passed.

Anna forgot to look at the clock and it was nearly seven when the last of the dishes had been collected and Dr Keslar and Sister, with Dr Lancing, went round the ward to check on each patient and bring the reports up to date before the night staff took over later.

'Nurse—can you get me a bowl to put my fruit in?'

Dr Keslar looked across at her as she brought one from the kitchen. Was there the hint of a conspiratorial smile in his hazel eyes? She felt an immediate lightness in her body, whatever it was that passed between them, straightening her aching shoulders after arranging the oranges and grapes, before saying goodnight to Sister and being told to go off duty at once.

Most of the heavy traffic had gone and she turned into the gate, enjoying her freedom. Except for the shopping. That was hard work, too, with Gran along. But tomorrow night would be fun. A girl's got to have some social life, even the more earthy kind, she told herself with a little wry smile, getting out to Shane's leaping welcome and her grandmother, wearing a pale blue knitted suit, her grey hair combed back becomingly, already waiting in the doorway.

'Oh—Gran . . .' Anna groaned, 'you make me feel positively grubby,' as she surveyed her own crumpled dress. 'I'll have to go and freshen up and change. You want to go now, do you?'

'Well—I thought we might eat when we get back, without hurrying. Unless you're very hungry . . .'

'No. Of course not. We'll only be an hour at the outside. Just give me a few minutes.'

Her legs ached as she climbed the winding stair-
way specially built for them, and was soon peeling
off her dress. Ten minutes later she reappeared
wearing well-cut beige slacks and a cream silk blouse,
for the sun was still golden across the fields and it
would be warm in the car and at the supermarket.

'I am so looking forward to seeing Ralph and Eve
again,' her grandmother said as they drove across
country.

'Me too, Gran.' They were almost there now.

'You're looking pale, Anna.'

'Mm. It's been a busy week—for everybody at the
hospital, Gran.'

'You haven't said much about your new doctor.'

'Um—he's nice. I like him.'

'Settled in, has he?'

Anna smiled as she brought the car to a stop in
one of the spaces. 'Very quickly. He's directly under
Mr Lonsdale, you see, and very assured and confident.'

'Consultant material, obviously. Ambitious?'

'Yes. I'd say so. He's a very good registrar.
Besides—I shouldn't think he's in too much hurry.
Practical experience in the theatre is so necessary for
absolutely years ... to become a surgeon of Mr
Lonsdale's standing, Gran.'

'I know that, dear. But are you quite so happy
working in outpatients?'

'What makes you ask that? I prefer being on the
wards, I suppose, because of the patient involvement
on a day-to-day basis.'

She didn't add that she had been on the point of
asking to be transferred permanently back to
Rowan, but only this last week had changed her
mind and Jane Forster wisely decided not to probe

further, although she had noticed a slight hesitation before Anna replied. As if she needed to get straightened out in her own mind first. So, something was bugging her grand-daughter and, in time, she would perhaps become a confidant, if and when Anna needed one. They had a good and precious rapport—those two, going back to her first remembered holidays spent at their Cornish home by the sea. When Grandpa had been there too.

She quickly stifled a sigh, a moment of nostalgia and longing for a part of her life which had gone by, as she followed the slim, confident young woman, already grabbing a trolley ahead of her and consulting her shopping list.

It was when they were almost finished that a man's voice caused Anna's head to jerk back and the adrenalin start a rush through her veins. Impossible. It couldn't be—yet her heart knew best and quickened its beat and she heard him repeat the question. An assistant, replenishing the shelves, answered,

'Smoked mackerel? Yes—it's right at the end of the fish counter.'

Anna saw him then. He looked vulnerable with a wire basket in his hand; different too—younger; in light blue slacks and a navy sweater. Something in his whole demeanour brought a softly curved smile to her lips. There was no way he could avoid seeing her, yet just for a moment he too looked as if he was dreaming. Perhaps it was her hair, loose about her shoulders or, like him, her casual clothes. But he soon broke into a delighted grin and in three strides reached her side.

'Hullo, there. Surely this has to be some form of retribution for something I've done,' he said grimly.

'There has to be another way. It's positively lethal among all these trolley things.'

She laughed sympathetically, shaking her head. 'I'm afraid it's a necessary chore if you want to eat. Fortunately, we don't have to do it too often.'

'Thank goodness for that. I shall have to plan things a little better for the future, but I've only just moved into my small flat and, with the weekend looming . . .'

He was eyeing Jane, who had now joined them, with some interest.

'This is my grandmother, Mrs Forster. Dr Keslar . . .' she said lightly.

'Really. I've heard about you . . .' Jane said, smiling happily.

'Oh—have you?' He glanced at Anna who felt her face pinking up before looking away. Then he went on, having noticed the blush with some satisfaction, 'This really is a hurly-burly, isn't it?' and moved out of the way of another trolley.

'Do you know,' Jane Forster broke in confidingly, 'I haven't heard anyone use that expression in years. Do you come from the West Country, Dr Keslar?'

He regarded her with a slightly amused expression. 'No, Mrs Forster. Wales, actually. My father still lives there.'

'I see.'

'I must get my shopping done. Have to get through before they close and I haven't eaten yet. There aren't enough hours in one day, are there Staff Nurse? Or is it Mrs Forster? It hadn't occurred to me that you might be . . .'

'She isn't married,' Gran broke in, 'and her name is Annabel. We call her Anna . . .'

While she was still recovering, her grandmother

went on imperturbably, 'Why don't you come back with us for supper, Dr Keslar? There's a chicken and mushroom casserole in the oven and plenty for all of us.'

Anna felt her senses reeling, she even closed her eyes, waiting for him to excuse himself politely, but firmly. Her grandmother's audacity had rendered her unable to speak. But a rather pleased-looking Paul Keslar was thanking her and accepting the invitation with enthusiasm.

'How kind of you. Did you know that I haven't unpacked properly yet and I haven't a clue where all the cooking things are. Not that I'm very adept with them but I'm willing to have a go.'

'Where do you have your flat?' Anna asked when she could sound reasonably calm. She hadn't dared look at Jane yet. That was to come.

'It's on the main road actually. A little village called Wilcombe.'

'Just a few minutes from where we live. Good. Then you can follow us when we leave,' Gran said calmly.

'If we don't finish our shopping Dr Keslar won't have time for his either,' Anna said firmly. Then, noticing his intent look as she went to move on after Jane, flitting from one side to the other, 'We will wait for you in the car park if we're first out. You *do* want to—don't you?'

'Yes. I do want to—very much . . .'

Her cheeks burned as her senses took over, so that she could no longer think clearly about the rest of the shopping. But her grandmother knew what was needed, checking now and then.

'Shall we have some cream, dear? I've got some raspberries defrosting and with a dash of brandy—

they'll be delicious. A special treat tonight.'

'What . . .' Anna said sternly, 'are we supposed to be celebrating, Gran?'

'I don't really know, dear. Do we have to have a reason? Besides—we do have a guest. I enjoy that, don't you?'

'Gran—hasn't it occurred to you that nurses just don't invite the doctors they work with home for a meal—especially when he's only just come here. Whatever will he think?'

'He looks very happy about it, and you didn't invite him, Anna. I did.'

CHAPTER THREE

He was already standing beside the green Citroen which was parked quite near to Anna's car, one arm resting nonchalantly on the roof, when she and Gran came out of the exit with their shopping. As soon as she was behind the wheel he waved and got into his own car, following her out of the forecourt and staying in view in her mirror the whole time.

She felt too bemused to say more, after that first burst of protest, which Gran had endured with stoicism.

Dusk was falling and Anna switched on her head-lights which was also a safety measure because of the many bends in the lane which wound its way between the fields. Then, signalling to the green car behind, she turned into the driveway, still disbelieving when he did the same. They had left an outside light on above the kitchen door, high up on the wall among a pink climbing rose, filled with early buds and looking lovely in the floodlighting.

Paul Keslar slammed his door and came to help carry in the overflowing bags of groceries, he and Gran already chatting away non-stop, while Anna went to close the five-bar white gate. The sight of Dr Keslar with his arms around two brown paper bags, crossing the lawn, was too much. She simply couldn't take in the unexpected happenings of the past two hours. Mervyn Abbot, chugging up the hill in a tractor, stopped and was about to say something until he saw Paul, then hesitated.

'Sorry. I didn't know you had company. It isn't your brother home, is it?'

'No. It's not Tim, Mervyn. Look—I'm so sorry. I must go, we haven't eaten yet. You're working awfully late too, aren't you?'

He shrugged and grinned, showing perfect white teeth. 'Always try to keep one day ahead, you know, and there won't be much work done tomorrow on the fields because of the evening. You will come, won't you, Anna?' His voice held a strong note of pleading.

'Of course. I promised. But I'm not sure how soon I can make it. I'll see you there. Night ... Must go ...'

She ran lightly over the lawn with Shane barking at her side to find Paul Keslar pouring sherry into three glasses at Gran's instigation. He looked quite at home, raising his eyebrows at Anna when she came into the dining end of the kitchen.

'Mrs Forster quite sweeps a man off his feet, doesn't she?' he grinned delightedly, something she hadn't seen before. 'Aren't I the lucky one tonight?' He moved deliberately around the table to her and handed her a glass.

She held out her hand, laughing, shaking her head, giving in to the situation.

'This ...' she told him, 'is all very unexpected, but if you're happy to be here, we're—glad to have you.'

'I couldn't have had a nicer welcome. Thanks,' he said, sipping his sherry and looking around at the beamed ceiling and white walls.

'This is delightful—what a pleasant place to be ...' he really meant it.

'Do sit down,' she said. 'Supper will only be a few

minutes. I'll just lay another place.' He watched as
she took another tablemat from the drawer and put
an extra chair for him. She felt a little tingling in
her spine and the inevitable colour rushing to her
face, wondering what his thoughts were, before going
to help as Gran came trundling the dinner wagon
through from the kitchen.

'You see . . .' she said proudly, 'I'm still needed
around here, even if it is only to show off my culinary
prowess.'

'It smells delicious . . .' Paul was the type of guest
she adored. 'I've never been inside an oast house
before,' he went on as they sat down. 'Whose idea
was it to convert it like this?' He was looking at
Anna while she took the lids from the pottery dishes.

'My father's actually, though Mum went along
with it too, of course.'

He looked up at the iron spiral staircase. 'I had
no idea one could do so much with it. Your parents
are away, I take it?'

'Yes. In Iceland. Would you like to help yourself?'

He was unable to resist an appreciative, 'Oh . . .'
when the lid was raised and the gorgeous smell of
chicken, mushrooms and herbs was released.

Then Gran, never at a loss for words, plunged
straight in. 'So where in Wales are you from, Dr
Keslar?'

'The name is Paul, Mrs Forster—how can we be
formal after a meal like this? I come from a village
at the foot of the Cambrian mountains. My father
had a country practice there but unfortunately he
has developed an illness which meant he was forced
to retire early. He was able to get me through medical college and is now able to stay at home, which is

something, because of extremely good care from a resident nurse-housekeeper who keeps me informed about his condition. I get up there as often as I can, of course. Now—tell me about Iceland. Have you ever been there? And can I call you Anna? Away from the hospital. Do you mind?' He had looked across at her suddenly.

'No. Of course not.' The quick smile which sprang to her eyes was not lost on Gran and, for Anna, a brief return of the chemistry, first experienced in the surgery, especially as Paul's eyes were slow to leave hers, as if there was something which had just occurred to him too.

There was a slight pause, almost a tangible one, before Gran persisted. 'Do you think you will like Calderbury, Paul?'

'I really haven't had time to get around it yet, Mrs Forster. It's very different from living in London, certainly. To begin with, I'm not used to the rural surroundings—and the hospital is a little— well—smaller, certainly.' He looked across the table again at the glow on Anna's hair, as she raised her eyes to answer his question. 'You must have found that too. I believe you came here from St Thomas's?'

She wondered how he knew that, as she said at once, 'Yes, to both questions. But I'm glad I decided to make the move now. I hope you will be too.' For whatever reasons, she thought.

He shrugged consideringly. 'I'm not sure that I can accept some of the deprivations at the Royal with too good a grace. It seems they are in dire need of many replacements, but it's too soon to have a true assessment yet, naturally. I like the atmosphere and the staff. Give me a month and I shall have got to know my patients too. Only, as we both know, ours is a coming and going profession and one dare not get too involved. It's marvellous when one can say, "You're cured—you don't need to come back anymore"—isn't it, Anna?'

He suddenly remembered Gran, listening and making no contribution to the conversation, and apologised. 'I'm sorry. Do forgive us—you must be very bored, Mrs Forster.'

'Not at all,' she said truthfully. 'I'm really enjoying this evening. Will you have some more coffee, Paul?'

'Please. Then I must go,' he glanced at his watch, as he spoke, then thanked Anna as she re-filled his cup. But now it was Gran who said, over his head,

'Was that Mervyn you were speaking to at the gate, dear?'

'Yes,' Anna said shortly. Why had Gran asked that question right at this moment?

'Sounds very rural when you speak of farm machinery,' Paul broke in, sensing Anna's discomforture, and not a little curious to know who Mervyn was. He too had seen the fair man leaning from his tractor towards Anna, quite possessively, and he had his own reasons for wanting to know how important he was to her.

Gran, explaining, said they were their nearest neighbours. With which point he had to be content.

As he left, he said to her, 'Thank you for inviting me back here with you. It was one of the nicest things to happen since I left London. I do appreciate it.'

'It was our pleasure,' she said gracefully, and meant it.

Then he looked at Anna, his expression unsmiling, almost intense. 'Won't you come to the gate with me and tell me which way I should drive back?'

'Of course. There's a quick way across country if you don't mind there being no lights anywhere.'

Outside, the lawns and flowerbeds were bathed in moonlight. Anna went ahead to open the gate for him, coming back to where he stood, waiting. There was a new and closer feeling between them now; a kind of intimacy in being just the two of them. Her face was pale in the moonlight, her hair full of soft moonglow, and for a moment he said nothing, just looked at her, then around at the tall trees, silently quivering, while above them was a ceiling of stars. He said reluctantly, 'Time to go, Anna. All this lovely quiet—how lucky you are to come back here after one of our gruelling days. I envy you . . .'

'I know. Especially when one leaves all those patients trapped in beds in the wards. Which, incidentally, is where I shall be this weekend. But Rowan is my ward actually.'

'Really? I'm on call too this weekend.'

'Goodnight . . .' she said softly, suddenly happy. She would see him tomorrow.

'Goodnight, Anna.' His hand closed over hers for a second, his touch physically imprinted, so that she was aware of her reaction for a long time afterwards. He slid into his seat and said teasingly, 'Hope I remember to call you "Staff" in the right places tomorrow. Goodnight—and thanks . . .'

She stood there in the darkness, leaning on the gate, until she could no longer hear his car engine; but looking from the back of the house across the fields she saw the headlights of it now and then as he emerged from between tall hedgerows and took the road which snaked across the flat country to join up with the one leading to the village where he had just moved in. Then she went thoughtfully into the house. Something had happened to her. She was falling in love with Paul Keslar in no uncertain way. Heavens—it was like sickening for something. All the symptoms manifesting themselves, one by one, until the spots came out and the condition had a name.

But it was hopeless. Or was it? Could he possibly be attracted too? Oh—it was all too much and she was reacting in a thoroughly immature fashion. So unlike her. She could never be manipulated into anything. But he wasn't doing that. Not consciously anyway. It was all in her own mind. It could lead nowhere; and she had better get both feet firmly planted on the ground again before things got out of hand. Only—nothing else could explain this inner compulsion to want to see him, be with him again, a day by day build up, until . . .

'In only just a few days?' she argued mindfully.

'From the first moment,' her conscious self answered. He was never a stranger from the time he turned into that corridor and their eyes met curiously before Mr Lonsdale introduced them. It was as if she had unknowingly been waiting for him. There was so much to say to each other which might never be said. She could love him so very much—his inner self, which was loving a man wholly, because physically there could be no doubt as to how much he moved her, set her pulses racing; even his fingers on her wrist had done that—so what if . . .?

She shivered deliciously as she ran her bath, relieved that he was quite unaware of her thoughts as he drove home. He would never know, of course, unless—but that was highly improbable. Tomorrow she would see him briefly and outwardly be the efficient staff nurse on Rowan Ward, with whom he liked working because he knew he could trust her, and because he had also enjoyed a pleasant meal in her home.

As she switched off her light after setting her clock for six next morning, she decided that for her own peace of mind she should keep her imagination under stricter control in future. At least, where the new senior registrar was concerned.

Next morning she walked right into an emergency on the ward.

'Cardiac arrest,' one of the night nurses said as she passed her wheeling a locker. The two other nurses were hurrying, doing things in double-quick time. The patients looked apprehensive and quite relieved to see her reassuring smile and be told that Mr Jones was going to be all right. After delivering two badly-needed bedpans she went along for a word with the young night sister who had been called from Regis and who was now back in her office.

She was rubbing her shoulders and Anna guessed rightly that she had manually manipulated and pummelled Mr Jones at first.

'Oh—Staff—how lovely to see you. You must have known . . .'

'Mr Jones?'

'He'll be okay now, I think. Fortunately, the patient in the next bed rang his bell pronto—and the team, though depleted, got here fast. They've taken him to I.C. just to be on the safe side, but we're terribly behind, I'm afraid.'

'Not to worry, Sister. We'll catch up. Nurse Watts and a junior are on their way up. Fortunately we're early this morning. We'll get the rest of them washed first.'

Routine jobs like making of beds and temperatures and patients' baths, for those who were the least bit mobile, were soon under way. The night staff went off and Anna was in charge until Sister came.

While breakfast was being dispensed, under the supervision of a temporary male nurse, she ran her eye down the report sheet, gone through earlier with Night Sister. Oh, dear—Emily had been playing up again. She was a long-term patient who had no-one at home to look after her and who flatly refused to go into a home where there was a warden in care. Every time it was suggested she was assailed by all manner of ailments; each one had to be investigated, or she would simply demand attention or resort to incontinence. Poor, lovable Emily.

After breakfast, the nurses gathered round Sister's table for a report on each patient and details of medication and special care. Sister, who had come on duty at nine, added her own comments when necessary, so each nurse was fully in the picture.

'Mrs Lawson is going to theatre at eleven. Mr Hughes thinks it can't wait until Tuesday, so her pre-med at ten, Staff. I hope she's had her bath. Mr Lathan will be going home sometime this afternoon. I have yet to contact his people. So, with Mr Jones gone to Intensive, we have two empty beds. Any questions?' She glanced round at their faces. 'Good. Go to it, then . . .'

Mrs Lawson was still wearing her own nightdress. Returning with her theatre gown and report, Anna drew the curtains, noting the patient's apprehensive state at the prospect of the op.

'Here's your exclusive Paris model . . .' she said brightly. 'I'm afraid you're going to have to slip that pretty pink one off for a while, but not for too long.

We'll have you looking gorgeous again when your husband comes in tonight. Let me help you.'

'I can manage, Nurse, if you're busy.'

'Good girl. I'll be back in a minute.'

She went quickly down the ward to prepare the pre-med injection, going to Sister's table as she was putting down the phone and beckoning to her.

'I'm a bit worried about Mr Coles, Staff. He's haemorrhaging again. Dr Keslar is coming in to see him. Will you see that he has everything ready?'

'Yes, Sister.'

'Oh—who can we send to theatre with Mrs Lawson? I can't possible spare you.'

'Nurse Miller is third year.'

'Of course. Delegate her for that then, will you? Oh—do the examination trolley yourself. Dr Keslar is very hot on everything being there to hand—and doesn't hesitate to say so.'

'I know . . .'

'I'd forgotten. You've been working with him in O.P. all week.'

Anna nodded. 'I'm giving Mrs Lawson her pre-med now. Then I'll get the trolley laid up.'

She wondered if her feet had gained wings as, glancing at the watch on her dress, she sped back up the ward to Mrs Lawson, checking that her wrist tabs were correct, that her dentures were out, that her report was up to date, before returning it to Sister's table, after suggesting that Mrs Lawson try to relax and have a lovely drowsy half hour.

Nurse Miller was checking a patient's saline drip when she stopped by the bed.

'Mrs Lawson's reports are on the table. Go with her to theatre at eleven. Dr Keslar's on his way to look at Mr Coles, so that's where I'll be for the next few minutes. Oh—and Mrs Keen is on an hourly B.P.-check. Dr Lancing had a chart written up. Can you do that or get the auxiliary to do it?'

She worked quickly, making sure that everything was on the trolley which should be there. Dr Keslar could be here at any moment now and she was not going to risk any of his disapproving glances when last night she had seen something of the kind of man he could be, relaxed, away from the hospital and oh—so very male and disturbing to her senses. And he had looked at her with much more than mere interest. As if he had wanted to kiss her. At that thought and her own day-dreaming, she pulled herself up sharply. It was inexcusable. She stood quite still, getting her thoughts into perspective, so that when he strode into the ward a few minutes later she had already drawn the curtains around Mr Coles's bed and the trolley was in readiness.

Dr Keslar looked preoccupied this morning, making straight for Sister's table. They went through Mr Coles's report notes and then came together to see him. Anna, hovering, saw him glance quickly at the trolley before he began to question his patient.

Sister turned back the sheet herself and Paul Keslar began his examination of the distended abdomen. Then he looked up.

'If you're very busy, Sister, I can manage with Staff Nurse, thank you.'

'Very well, Dr Keslar—if that's all right with you.'

He nodded without looking up. 'Quite,' and to Anna who stood by the bed, 'Just there, Nurse, if you will. Ah, that hurts, Mr Coles, does it?' His patient had winced under the gently probing fingers and the registrar made his decision. Standing up, regarding him thoughtfully, he chose his words carefully. Some patients could be put in the picture completely, preferring it that way, and there were the others who definitely could not. Anna was not at all surprised when Paul said lightly, 'There is some soreness, Mr Coles, so we must give it a little longer to heal up. The bleeding seems to have stopped for now. I'll get Sister to give you something for the pain. Try to get some sleep. You didn't have much last night, did you?'

'It was a dreadful night . . .'

'Yes. Well, I'll be back to see you again later. I think he could do with another pillow, Staff Nurse, don't you?'

'I'll fetch one . . .'

'Come over to Sister's table first. I'd like a word as you'll probably be on duty by yourself this afternoon.'

'Does that mean—you'll be in later?'

'Yes. I think so.'

He explained to them in medical terms what he suspected.

'I want to talk to Mr Lonsdale before we proceed further, but I think we have no alternative but to operate,' he finished. 'Meanwhile, I'll keep an eye on him today and tomorrow, as Mr Lonsdale is away for the weekend.'

Anna excused herself then as Sister wanted to talk to him about another patient. She was taking out the extra pillow for Mr Coles when she heard his footsteps in the corridor and as she closed the door of the linen room he was there, waiting. Her pulses raced in spite of herself as she hugged the pillow in her arms, her eyes raised to his, unerringly. She could do nothing to prevent it, because he had come to find her.

'I'd like to take you out for a meal later tonight, Anna. Can you suggest somewhere?'

'I—can't tonight,' she said, her disappointment showing. 'I've promised to go to the barbeque and country-and-western dance in the village. It's in aid of the Scanner. I must go . . . I'm sorry . . . really—I am.'

'With your farmer friend? The one at the gate last night. I didn't realise that I was butting in.'

'Perhaps another time,' she said forlornly.

He looked at her sceptically, his head on one side. 'Perhaps. We'll see.'

Then he was gone, leaving her clutching at Mr Coles's pillow, before walking resolutely back into the ward.

When he was more comfortable, she left the other nurses to grab a quick cup of coffee, returning to see the auxiliary coming to bed four to take Mr Neale's B.P. Then she ran her eyes along the beds to check which dressings needed doing. Mrs Lawson lay half asleep under her sheets. It was just on eleven. She would be going down soon. Then she gasped and hurried to bed four, taking over from the trainee nurse.

'What on earth do you think you're doing?'

'Taking his B.P. You said—every hour.'

'You haven't been doing it on his right arm?'

'No. Not last time.'

'Can't you see he's had an incision? There are twelve stitches on that upper arm. Are you blind, Nurse? Sorry, Mr Neale.'

'I told her that was my bad arm . . .' he muttered. 'She said it didn't matter, but it hurt like hell. Jolly glad you came along.'

'No harm done,' she said with more confidence than she was feeling, as she released the tubing and wrote on his chart, not surprised to find it was still up a bit.

Her voice was sharper than the student nurse had heard it previously, as she came into the kitchen at her request.

'Do you realise you could have given him a thrombosis?' she asked, facing her across the table. 'I can't see you becoming a nurse unless you use your brain a bit more. Now I can't trust you to do any-thing . . .'

'It doesn't matter. I'm leaving at the end of the month, don't you know? Got another job to go to. I'm fed up with nursing. I don't think I'll be any good at it . . .'

'I couldn't agree more,' Anna said icily. 'Meanwhile, you can clear up the sluice and fill the water jugs. I'll have a word with Sister about getting you relieved as soon as possible.'

A fracas like that one upset her more than showed on the surface. As she went back to the ward, Mrs Lawson's trolley passed and she turned back to ask the junior to get her bed re-made at once. She couldn't go wrong with that, surely. Then, seeing that Sister had gone back to her table and was sitting with a phone at one ear, writing quickly while she listened, she consulted her own list and went to check a transfusion tube which looked suspect.

A plaintive, 'Nurse, can you open a window? It's stuffy in here,' was met with a playful, 'It's a lovely airy ward but I will if you're sure the rest of you aren't in a draught.' Still from the same woman, detaining her with her hand on Anna's bare arm, 'Pour me some orange juice, Nurse. There's a full bottle to be opened in my locker.'

She complied as quickly as possible, keeping her patience under control, and went to peep at Mr Coles before fetching the diet sheets. Already the trolley was outside in the corridor and the noise of cutlery and china disturbing the quiet. She would never be through before lunch at this speed and was relieved to see Nurse Miller back from the theatre.

'What's next, Staff?'

'Lunch, I should think. Get washed up and we'll start ladling out the soup. I think we can manage without the junior. I've put her on sluice duty.'

'Oh, dear. Well, she is a bit careless. I'd hate to see hot soup upset over the patients. It smells like chicken today.'

'It is,' Anna said, lifting the lids, her mood dispelled as she checked the menu list for the items patients had previously ticked for their choice, provided they were not on a strict diet. Mealtimes were not one of her favourite routine tasks of the day. Not an enjoyable experience and one requiring great tact, especially if something ran out and had to be substituted for something else. Then the grumbles began, and diplomacy won.

It seemed a long time since she had eaten breakfast that morning. She knew better than to attempt to face a day without it, but now she was hungry too, having used up a lot of energy that morning. If only she could have said 'Yes' to Paul Keslar's invitation. It would really be something to look forward to that evening; a real shot in the arm stimulus. But, when ladling rice pudding and peaches into never-ending dishes, Nurse Miller asked her if she was doing anything, it being Saturday, it was nice to be able to answer, 'Yes—I'm going to a barbecue.'

'Lucky you. I'm staying in to wash my hair. My boy friend is away on a course. Anyway, I'm too tired to do much when I get home. It's too late usually.'

Half way through the afternoon, while Sister was taking her two hours off duty, Anna picked up the phone when it rang and, at the same time, saw Paul coming down the ward, heading for her table. He waited, his back to her, looking from the window, while she spoke to Mr Lawson who was enquiring about his wife.

'She's in the recovery room, yes—the operation is over. No—not this afternoon; perhaps for a little while this evening. Oh, yes—she's fine. Goodbye.'

How vulnerable the back of his head looked to her in that moment before he turned and came to give her the reports he had taken with him. She knew quite well, and so did he, that they could have been sent by hand by someone else.

'No problems?'

'I don't think so,' she answered lightly, while her heart belied her words, stepping up its beating while he stood so near. 'Mr Coles seems to have stabilised.'

'Yes. I noticed that he's still asleep. Right. In that case, I'm off now. I saw Dr Lancing cross the precinct a moment ago and I want to have a word with her before she goes out again. I—hope you enjoy your barbecue. Sounds interesting.'

Anna went slowly to the window after his white coat disappeared. Minutes later she saw him emerge and walk quickly towards the separate building where the nurses had rooms; the top floor was given over to three flats. Dr Lancing had one of these.

His dark suit made him look even more distinguished, she thought unhappily—the dividing line more apparent. He crossed between the flower beds of wall flowers and late tulips, ducking his head under the dripping laburnum tree, yellow in the sunshine of the afternoon, and disappeared into the wide oaken door of the nurses' home. She pictured him, taking the stairs two at a time, until he reached the third floor.

Then, straightening her back and giving herself a sharp, disciplinary nudge, Staff Nurse Forster glanced quickly down each side of her ward, saw that most of the patients were busily chatting to their visitors, sent the trainee nurse to collect the flowers and put them in water before she went resolutely into the ward kitchen and, switching on the kettle, made herself a cup of coffee, before going back to her table to catch up on her notes for Sister's return at five-thirty.

CHAPTER FOUR

IT was after seven when Anna turned into the gate of the Oast House and went towards the kitchen door, almost absent-mindedly bending to run her fingers through Shane's long coat in answer to his noisy welcome.

The last thing she felt like doing tonight was joining the happy, jigging throng inside that barn. Yet usually it was the community spirit among the villagers which she most enjoyed. It was the nitty-gritty of folk, the genuine help-your-neighbour thing among them. She couldn't chicken out. Perhaps after a bath and a change of clothes, when she could finally leave the hospital atmosphere with her print dress and belt, it would be better.

But oh—how delightful it would have been if she were meeting Paul instead. She knew exactly what she would have worn and where she would have suggested they go to dine. Pollards—not too expensive, but good food, exquisitely served—where they could have sat through the whole evening if they had felt like it in one of the alcoves, pink table lamps reflecting softly their relaxed mood. While she learned more about him, she could have forgotten that he was Mr Lonsdale's deputy and she a nurse. They would have been just a man and a woman and, before the night was over, she would have known if he felt any of the things she did. *Oh Paul, what are you doing to me? Have you any idea?* Yet—he had wanted to take her out—he would most certainly not have suggested it otherwise. It wasn't just a return for the supper they gave him last night. If so—he would have invited Gran along too. Instead, there would be sausages around a barbecue and lots of plonk and cider. Oh, well, she had better get ready. Gran seemed occupied with a friend for the evening, entertaining tonight in her own apartment, so she was quite free.

After a quick, refreshing bath she slipped into a cotton dress with tiny green flowers and cream sandals, slung a cream woollen coat around her shoulders and started out once more, only this time in the opposite direction.

It was still golden across the fields and surrounding countryside, and she could now hear the music as she turned into the already-peopled field with the various attractions, for they were out to make a sizeable amount of money tonight for the Body Scanner, much needed in this part of the country.

She saw Mervyn already approaching the moment she had parked. He came towards her over the tufted grass, looking fair and handsome—no other words to describe him—his blue shirt the colour of his eyes, and grey tailored pants emphasising his lean muscled body.

He took her keys and locked her car door unable, indeed, not attempting, to conceal his delight at seeing her.

'I was afraid you weren't going to make it,' he confessed, slipping his hand through her arm possessively as they began to walk towards the barn.

'I said I would . . .'

'I know, but . . .'

'So . . . I'm here,' she said, laughing up at him,

flattered and touched, in spite of her other thoughts. 'No more buts—I feel like enjoying myself—letting my hair down.'

'You have, and I like it.'

Her hair, soft and gleaming, curled on to her shoulders tonight. It matched her mood.

'Are you tired?'

'Not now. Besides—that's no question to ask a lady—what a compliment!'

'You know I didn't mean—well—you have been working all day.'

'So have you. Someone had to make the inside of the barn look so attractive. And all the lights—it's lovely.'

'Oh. It's a communal effort. Would you like a drink first?'

'Please.'

'Sherry? Something long, or over here—our special—mother's mead wine?'

'No—thanks very much.' She knew what effect mead was supposed to have on one. 'Sherry would be fine.'

'I see—playing safe . . .' he said teasingly, then found her a seat at one of the small tables to be used later when the cooking got under way. She remembered her own contribution then.

'Mervyn. Sausages and chops—in the car. I'll get them.'

'Later will do. Just sit there and relax and let's talk. We never seem to have time to talk, do we? And . . . you're very nice to look at tonight, Anna.'

'Thank you. So are you.'

She knew at once that she should not have started the evening this way. She felt a little reckless, perhaps because the gay mood was forced, she hoped this way to make it less so as the evening progressed. Besides, it was a kind of palliative, except that now, seeing his eyes darken and his expression tense slightly, she knew that he was taking her words seriously, reading more into them than she intended, which could only lead to further disillusionment sometime. Yet he was such good company and really wanting to please her. No woman could fail to appreciate his efforts to make her feel special to him.

A cool breeze blew across the field, making her reach for her coat, and she suggested they go inside for a time. He leapt to his feet with alacrity then and his hand on her bare arm was comforting. She enjoyed their first dance, slipping into his arms naturally, going on until the music stopped for the interval and they were both hot and breathless.

She was relaxed now, gathered up into the festival mood of the evening. Her face, flushed and smiling, didn't resist when, slipping an arm around her shoulders, he kissed her lightly against her ear before guiding her through the crowd towards the entrance.

'I think we need some air . . .' he said softly. 'It's gruelling in here. Are you hungry yet? Another drink?'

She didn't answer—she couldn't—her heart seemed to somersault and, glancing at her, his eyes followed hers until he saw the two newcomers in the open entrance, who obviously found it impossible to come in when everyone else was trying to go out.

'Friends of yours?' he asked Anna as they moved closer, half recognising her guest of last night.

'Dr Lancing . . .' she said, introducing them, 'and—Dr Keslar; Mervyn Abbot, a—friend of mine. In fact, his parents have loaned this barn and field for the barbecue . . .'

'That's really why we're here,' Dr Lancing had noticed nothing unusual and looked extremely attractive in a cream dress with a soft neckline and a gold chain, her dark hair loose and turned under. Anna also recognised the French perfume she was wearing and knew she couldn't hope to compete now, or ever, even if she wanted to, against this simple sophistication.

'How did you know about it?' Mervyn asked them as they came out into the night under a sky thick with stars now.

'Paul—Dr Keslar—saw a notice on the board. In aid of the Scanner, isn't it? We thought it might be fun. It was a bit difficult to find but the people at the pub down the lane directed us. We heard the band and saw the lights anyway—and smelled the food. I'm really hungry now . . .'

'Then,' Mervyn said indicating the glowing charcoals, 'why don't we all get started. What would you like, Anna?'

'Anything . . .' was all she could manage, remembering her sausages still in the car.

'Why don't we all go and get our own?' she said on impulse.

'Yes.' Dr Lancing was already making her way towards the table. 'Come along, Paul . . .' she called over her shoulder. 'Just look at all that lovely sizzling food. Hunks of home-baked bread too—gorgeous.'

He entered into the whole thing completely then, dragging Anna to her feet so that she too had no choice but to do the same. They were next to each other, spearing sausages, while Mervyn and Dr Lancing were piling up their plates further along when, overcome with unexplained emotion, she stole a glance at his face, only to find that he was watching her, his eyes thoughtful in the glow. Neither of them spoke but Anna felt the same spear-like thrust through her body which happened each time their eyes did this. Still they didn't speak as they went back to the table where the other two were already eating. She had never felt at such a loss for words. Had he chosen to come here tonight deliberately? Was it just a chance opportunity to see her and whom she was with? Did it matter that much? How could it, when he was with someone like Dr Lancing? Unless he was using her; but he wasn't like that? Yet he had asked her out first. So why should she feel at such a disadvantage coupled with the other's glamorous looks? But she did feel so, just the same.

She was very conscious of him, amusedly watching Mervyn and Dr Lancing having a whale of a time as they chattered between mouthfuls of hot sausages and chicken legs. Then, as he sat down quite close to her, spreading mustard on his sausages before he spoke, there was that same feeling that she'd had at the hospital when they worked together, anticipating his thoughts. She wasn't surprised when he said,

'We didn't mean to gate-crash, Anna. It seemed a good idea when we decided to come, but I'm not so sure. I do hope we haven't spoiled your evening. You aren't annoyed, are you?'

'Why should I be? Oh—surely I haven't given that impression . . .'

'Not to anyone else, I imagine, but I see now why you had to refuse my invitation. He's nice—I like him—you look good together.' He put his hand on hers. 'I hope this doesn't mean that we'll be losing you, at the Royal . . .'

She was still trying to think of a way to tell him

that there was nothing between her and Mervyn as yet, nor could be, when Dr Lancing called to him.

'Paul—be a dear and fetch my coat from the car. It's a bit chilly . . .'

He put his plate down at once and took his car keys from the pocket of his beige trousers as he walked off.

Anna felt quite deflated now. She longed to go after him. To be alone with him. To talk. Just the two of them. To be near him. She wanted—oh— what did she want? Instead, there was this awful build-up of resentment that it was Dr Lancing and not herself, spending time with him tonight, when it could have been so different.

Then almost immediately she felt sorry—because Mervyn had been trying so hard to make her evening enjoyable and here she was, hankering after another man and she didn't know where she stood with him either.

He was coming back, wearing a heavy cream sweather now. She watched as he held Dr Lancing's coat for her and saw the look she gave him as she smiled up into his face.

Then Mervyn came.

'What are you doing over here by yourself?' he asked concernedly. 'Come on over to the fire. You see—you just can't get away from the hospital, can you? I'm glad they dropped in though. A good turn out, wasn't it? We must have taken quite a bit of money tonight.'

The four of them stood around the fire talking animatedly, their faces lit by the dancing flames of the huge bonfire, until people started to drift away, cars starting up, lighting the lane with their head-lights.

Mervyn asked Anna if she wanted to dance anymore. She shook her head. 'I don't think so. I've enjoyed it out here under the stars.'

From the barn the strains of country and western music still created the background for everything else in character with it.

'It's out of this world,' Dr Lancing said sincerely. 'I didn't know people still cared enough to do this sort of thing any more—with so much enthusiasm. You have a marvellous community thing going in this village.'

'Never a dull moment—always something coming up on the calendar,' he answered her, with teeth gleaming white in the darkness. 'It's work or play—mainly work; except that we do know when to switch off.'

'So I've observed,' Paul spoke carefully. 'I think we must go too. If you're ready, Erika; you're on call tomorrow too, aren't you?'

So that was her name. Was his voice different when he said goodnight to Anna? The tiniest inflection of softness? Had she imagined it? Because that was what she wanted most of all. To be someone special to him, in every way.

Watching their car join the others, she made a conscious effort to resist the temptation to follow them with her thoughts. She was here with Mervyn. He had moved closer, lifting her chin, wanting to know why she had gone silent.

'I must go too . . .' she murmured.

'Not yet . . .' his voice sounded husky, deep, with a build up of something she could only imagine. Then it registered fully. Mervyn was serious about her and expecting some response. She knew it for certain when he propelled her closer to him in a firm grip and searched for her mouth in the darkness. It simply hadn't occurred to him that she was leaving him so abruptly, by choice.

'I'm taking you home tonight. You know I want to, don't you?'

'I—I've got my car . . .'

'No problem about that. I can walk back.'

'But—won't they be needing you here? To help take everything down and get back to normal. They'll miss you.'

'So what? There are enough of them to lend a hand. Besides—they'll know where I am and that I'll be back sometime.'

She didn't want to hurt him, but there was no easy way, she decided, as they began to walk towards her car. His arm still kept her captive against his shoulder.

When they came to it she gently disengaged herself, but he pulled her closer, almost roughly, with more strength than he knew, his muscular arms like iron bands as his mouth searched desperately to find hers. She tried to twist away but it was no use. His passion, unbridled for a moment, hurt her with its intensity; his body hard against hers. She knew she had moved him and regretted it, because although his kiss was deeply long and bruising, it did nothing to her emotions. She remained passive until he let her go. Then she touched her bruised lips as she looked up at him in the moonlight.

'I'm—sorry,' she whispered.

'You don't have to be,' his voice shook but he went on. 'You don't feel the same way, Anna. I should have seen that. *I* should apologise, not you, and I do. I—hope I haven't spoiled the rest of the evening. It's just that——Oh, hell . . .'

'No. It was a good evening,' she shivered.

'You're okay?'

'Yes.'

'Anna—is there some other guy?'

'I think so.'

'I see. I—wish I'd known. Goodnight. You do want to go alone? You're sure?'

She nodded. 'Yes.'

But her hands on the wheel were unsteady and when a rabbit ran across in the beam of her head-lamps, she braked quickly and went on again with double concentration, relieved when she saw the light in the wall and turned into her home.

Gran was already in bed, so she could slip up to her own room with her thoughts, which were very mixed as she got ready for bed. It had been quite a day and she was probably over-tired, stretched emo-tionally, which seemed to be the case when, after putting out her light, sleep evaded her and her brain seemed filled with thoughts like a regiment of soldiers marching through. She couldn't meet Mervyn like that again. But how would she have responded if Paul Keslar had kissed her that way? The tingle in her spine told her the answer to that.

She was a fool. It was Erika Lancing who knew what his goodnight kisses were like. She willed her thoughts to stop there, annoyed that she was even tempted to invade another person's privacy. But at least she had been honest with Mervyn. They both knew where they stood now and she wouldn't accept any more invitations in future which might compli-cate things further. She didn't for one moment think he was really in love with her. Much more just a passing infatuation or even a physical reaction from the build up of the past weeks. She wouldn't want just anyone to kiss her—but if ever Dr Keslar did, she knew it would be devastating.

It was nothing new, this one-sided situation. More nurses than not felt a strong admiration for a doctor with whom they were in close contact. It was a special relationship, unspoken, sometimes un-recognised, but her own deep feelings told her that what she was feeling for Paul was very special indeed, also he must never know about it. Which thought left her with relief of a kind. It also meant that she was in for some moments of acute de-spondency when momentary longings might under-mine her efficiency if she didn't guard against it. Having decided all of this in her mind and reached her conclusions, she slept dreamlessly and awoke quite refreshed, much to her surprise, just as the alarm bell tingled beside her bed. She was out in the woods with Shane twenty minutes later, before coming back, eating a good breakfast and, because it was Sunday, leaving Gran undisturbed.

Both Dr Lancing and Dr Keslar were on call today, but he wasn't brought in unless really needed. Sundays were a little different on the ward; a more relaxed atmosphere prevailed. It was one of the con-fiding days when sometimes patients felt more homesick than other days and unburdened their-selves a little. One just needed more time to listen. Anna didn't mind in most cases, especially if she was able to offer a reassuring word in the right place. But this morning one of the male patients was defin-itely feeling very low. He sat by his bed wearing a deep blue towelling robe which his wife had brought in the previous day.

'Roll up your sleeve, Robert,' she said. 'I just want to take your B.P. What a gorgeous dressing-gown.'

'It's an early birthday present . . .'

'You're not too worried about tomorrow's op, are you?' She saw at once that he was depressed. 'Your wife has perfect taste . . .'

'I know. She thinks I'm wearing this on holiday in August—Spain we've booked for.'

'Oh. Well you still could be, you know.'

He shook his head wordlessly.

'Bit bothered?'

'Worried sick, Nurse.'

He rolled down his sleeve while she brought his chart up to date. Anna, putting a hand on his shoulder, felt him trembling beneath her touch.

'This won't do, you know. You'll be all right. Professor Beard is doing it, isn't he?'

'It's not that. You see—she doesn't know there's a growth there. She thinks it's just an ulcer; which is what they thought in the beginning.'

'But—she would have been told after the X-rays showed . . .'

'No. I asked the Professor not to tell her.'

'I see.'

'She worries over everything so. Even small things. She couldn't take it.' .

'Have you got any children?'

'Two. A boy and girl. They both need new school clothes because they'll be going to different schools after the holidays. Kay thinks I'll be back at work in three or four weeks. But I won't, will I? I don't get sick pay either. We've just had a new carpet and a three-piece suite so there's not much in the kitty. I just don't know how I'm going to tell her, Nurse.'

'Why not let one of the doctors do it? She will have to know sometime. Is she coming in today?'

'They all are and they won't be expecting to see me like this either. It will be a shock.'

He was on a saline drip after an exploratory examination the previous day.

'It won't hurt them to worry about you for a change,' she said firmly. 'Your B.P. is up because you're getting in a state. Now you are the patient and you must rest today. They'll work it out. Would you rather they didn't come?'

'Oh, no. I want to see them. It's just . . .'

'I know. But you won't have to tell them anything, Robert. After tomorrow, someone will have a word with your wife and put her in the picture and she'll know as much as you do. Then you can talk between yourselves. You know—that really is a lovely blue . . .' she said over her shoulder as she left him to reflect. She herself meant to have a word in Dr Keslar's ear when next she saw him.

Meanwhile, two new patients were waiting for beds in the day room, having been admitted for minor routine ops for next day. She was standing with her head on one side, considering the bed situation, when she heard his voice.

'Leave a memo for me, will you?' to someone in the corridor. The next moment he came into the ward and she tried to still her racing heart, breathing deeply while she waited at the table for him to join her. His face was inscrutable. He was in no hurry as he pulled out a chair and asked if he might sit down.

Then he said very softly, 'Hullo . . .' and before she could decide if it had been specially pitched for her, he was saying,

'I just want to bring these notes up to date. Been to see Mrs Jones. I think you might be getting her back from Regis if Mr Lonsdale agrees to have her leg re-done. You have two beds I see, or was that what you were pondering on when I came in?'

'Yes. I also have two new patients.'

'Oh! Do you have tomorrow's list handy?'

She took it from a drawer and gave it to him. Then she told him of her conversation with Robert Gray.

All the time they were talking she could see how genuinely interested he was in his patients. Also, he approved of the way she had handled it.

'All right. I'll have a word—leave it with me. No other problems?'

'Nothing I can't cope with, hopefully.'

'Good.' His smile was enough to send her senses reeling, but fortunately he was already going over to Mr Coles's bed, sitting himself casually down on it while he looked at his charts.

Next, Anna went to assure the two new patients, a man and woman, that they were about to be 'put to bed'. It was a traumatic experience having to come into hospital, without feeling that just possibly you had been forgotten.

'I have to get one bed moved up and the other down into the men's section,' she explained. 'As you see, we have a sort of dividing panel, but now that another nurse is back we can get you settled in. Would you like some tea?'

'Yes, please, Sister,' they said gratefully.

She corrected them smilingly. 'I haven't quite reached those exalted heights yet,' she said. 'I'm Staff Nurse Forster. Sister will be here in the morning.'

She left them, perched on the edge of their chairs, suitcases beside them. Only this was not exactly a holiday. At least they had made friends and had already exchanged symptoms, and also fears.

Later, when they were in dressing gowns, sitting beside their beds, Dr Lancing came, her dark hair piled on top of her head today, wearing an open-necked cream silk shirt under her white coat.

'I've come to examine the two new patients, Staff Nurse.'

What an attractive smile she has, Anna thought, reliving the scene of last night as she pointed them out and left her to draw the curtains around their beds.

With one eye on the clock, she delegated various things to be done now that there were three of them on duty until seven-thirty.

'Urine and weighing for both new patients,' and so it went on. She had seen Robert's family leave so she had a quick word with him before sitting down at her table to make out even more reports and notes for when she went off duty herself.

Dr Keslar had left now. Unless it was something the house doctors couldn't handle, he would not be back until the morning. Then she would be working with him in out-patients, just as last week, except that perhaps this time Mr Lonsdale would expect her to stay with him.

But next morning as she and Jill Slade were preparing for day clinic as usual, the phone rang on the desk and she learned that she had been transferred back to Rowan and was to report there at once.

'I'm back on Rowan, Jill.'

'Oh, no. Who's coming here?'

'I am.' Susie was third year, dark skinned and very efficient. 'I haven't yet met the new senior registrar. What is he like to work with?' She had a lovely slow drawl.

'He's—nice,' Anna told her, 'but he's very much on the ball. For heaven's sake make sure everything is ready for him and—he likes you to be around—all the time.'

'Well—thank you. I look forward to meeting this perfect man . . .'

'He's not perfect,' Anna told herself as she went along the corridors and into the wards wing; 'but he is rather special.'

Then, looking ahead, she saw him coming towards her. Her head went back as she brought her thoughts under control. He stopped. 'Aren't you going in the wrong direction this morning?' he asked gently.

'No. I'm assigned to Rowan today, and probably all the week.'

'Oh. So that is that . . . I'll miss you.'

He was gone, turning the corner before she took one step towards her waiting ward full of patients.

When Sister touched her arm as she was pulling curtains back around a bed later and whispered, 'Come and have your coffee with us, Staff . . .' she went with some relief.

Dr Lancing put her head around the door a few minutes afterwards, asking, 'Can I beg one too?'

'Of course. Staff will get you one, won't you? We'll be lucky to have time to drink it though.'

Anna, coming back with the filled coffee cup, was just in time to hear Dr Lancing coming to the end of Saturday evening's barbecue. 'But you should see Staff's boy friend—or is he your fiancé, Staff? I could easily fall for him myself, Sister. He's magnificent.'

'Really, Staff? You're not leaving me to get married, I hope. I've just asked for you back here again permanently.'

'There's no question of that,' Anna said seriously.

'He isn't even my boy friend. Just a neighbour.'

'Oh . . .' Erika Lancing was obviously impressed. 'He told me that his father foots the bill for the Country and Western band and supplies most of the chicken free because it's in aid of the Scanner. In gratitude for his wife being cured of cancer two years ago. There's a lovely old farmhouse where they live, behind the village. I really must go that way again sometime. Without Dr Keslar though—because he thought that he and I were—closer than we are . . .'

Anna took their cups back to the kitchen wondering just what Mervyn would say if he knew that he was being discussed in Sister's office and by the attractive Dr Lancing. But overall—it was something of a relief to her own rather confused thoughts, to hear Dr Lancing talking so casually, in that 'all girls together' way.

CHAPTER FIVE

TIM came home from university and for Anna it was a relief to find him there most evenings when she arrived back from the hospital. They had always been good for each other; stimulating company, and now they were interested in each other's study and work too. It was nice to have a man about the house. He relieved her of some of the more menial tasks which were too much for Gran and fell to Anna usually. In three weeks' time he would be doing some practical work in a hospital for the summer, but he had elected to go further afield than the Royal, and in less than a week their parents would be flying home, so it was to be a real family reunion and Anna was already making preparations for them.

Nothing else had changed. The highlights of her working day were when Paul came on to the ward, or they met accidentally along the shiny corridors or elsewhere. He was involved in several training projects now, and making quite a name for himself among the medical staff, and, she suspected, being invited around socially to their homes. Certainly, he had dined with Mr Lonsdale, because Jill Slade had heard them discussing it. In some ways, she felt him to be a little out of reach; there was a definite dividing line to which she adhered, as she would with any other senior doctor. But, close to him physically, while he was examining a patient in the tiny space behind the bed curtains, or sometimes, if she was writing at her table and didn't hear him until the swish of his white coat behind her made her look up and feel her heart jump, or even to pass him, talking to another doctor, knowing he saw her but couldn't speak just then, was enough to send her emotions scattering for a brief moment. The pride she felt in him—her heart seemed to be bursting with it when someone spoke in his praise in her hearing. He must surely see the shine in her eyes when she had to look at him, listening to instructions or comments. Discussing one of the patients gave her an almost intimate feeling, because he always spoke gently and behaved as if she were his equal, giving her intelligence and opinion full reign.

But he kept it there, on the straight dividing line, because now he naturally thought of her, if at all outside the hospital, as spending her time with Mervyn Abbot, and he was a man any woman would find all male, and very attractive—so why should she need anyone else? There was no way he could suspect that her personal emotions were directed towards himself. She would hate him to know. She didn't go to any of the nurses' dances or discos because there were other things she preferred to do instead. Besides, she wouldn't go without a partner, and she could never ask Mervyn to take her now, after what had happened.

As Sister was back she felt entitled to ask for three days of overdue leave which was granted at once. So next morning, she and Tim were sitting in the latticed bay window of a coffee shop in Calderbury, having just chosen their mother's birthday present for Sunday, when Tim, hearing her catch her breath involuntarily, looked through the window to see a man wearing a cream silky shirt and beige pants, stop, hesitate, then come inside, looking around the door at Anna in undisguisedly pleased recognition.

'Anna—oh—sorry . . . You're with someone,' he said innocently. 'I didn't notice . . .'

'My brother, Timothy. This is Dr Keslar, Tim. He is Senior Surgical Registrar at the Royal. You aren't intruding—why don't you have coffee with us, Paul?'

It was the first time she had called him that and he noticed, but gave no other sign than to look pleased about something—or it may just have been because he had been invited to join them. But Tim noticed, not knowing that it had slipped out unknowingly.

'Well—in that case—I'd like to,' he said, seating himself opposite her. He really has the most unaffected, spontaneous smile, she thought, when he isn't looking serious or absorbed. She was very proud to introduce him to her brother, which fact Tim also noted. Anna had known instinctively that Paul had been curious about her male companion, even withdrawn, until he discovered his relationship to her. This fact gave her spirits another upward lift. Was it possible he cared—just a little?

Paul was gentle with Tim who, halfway through medical school, had reached the stage when he thought he 'knew it all'. But, including her in their conversation, gave her an opportunity to tactfully smooth out the edges and she saw by Paul's expression that he had been through it all himself and remembered. Then Tim was telling him that their parents were flying home next day.

He turned to Anna. 'Are you really having a full weekend off-duty too?'

'Yes. I'll be back on Monday.'

'I'm off too. Tomorrow I'm visiting some friends

at Rye. Do you know it?'

She shook her head.

'Oh . . .' he went on, 'I think you'd love it. It's the only unspoiled town left. Fascinating. It's an hour's run from here. Maybe, sometime, I could take you . . .'

She was surprised and terribly elated. 'I'd like that . . .' she said simply. 'I do hope you have a good day.'

It wasn't at all what she had meant to say. It sounded inadequate. She was also aware of Tim's raised eyebrows; looking from one to the other with an amused grin, however slight; she knew what he was thinking, and that he would return to the subject of Dr Keslar later, having rumbled something he hadn't known about.

He did. On the drive back. She had deliberately kept a low profile as they left the coffee shop together, but going in opposite directions when they had directed Paul to the shop he was looking for at the other end of town.

Anna had walked thoughtfully back to their car, through the narrow, cobbled streets, musing happily for a little while as she wondered what they might have said to each other if she had been having coffee alone. Two missed opportunities. Tim, hearing her sigh, asked about Dr Keslar and their work at the hospital, surprised that she often had to stand in for Sister in charge. He saw her eyes soften, noticed the animation in his sister's voice at the mention of the doctor and probed a bit more until she stopped suddenly and asked why he wanted to know so much about him.

'No—he isn't married. Why?'

'I was just wondering if he should happen to be

my prospective brother-in-law,' he said laconically, giving her a sly side glance.

'Of course not. Nothing of the kind. We simply both work on surgical, that's all.'

'I only asked. Is he clever?'

'He's marvellous . . .' she said softly. 'Do you know, Tim; they say in theatre, that when he operates, he sews like a woman turning in a seam— so neatly—such small stitches—I haven't seen him operate yet. Maybe I will sometime. I'd really like to.'

Their parents arrived late next day, driving down from the airport in a hired car, both excited and thrilled to be home again.

Eve Forster was still a slim and elegant woman, her hair not yet greying, and it was easy to see whom Anna took after. For the first hour she barely stopped talking, while Ralph Forster, grey haired, lithe and strong still, was quieter, more thoughtful, as Anna was too. He soon disappeared with Shane to roam around the house and garden, disappearing into the woods, revelling in this very English way of life he would return to some day.

The days passed too quickly. Tim had already left for his practical training and Anna, arriving home from the hospital one evening, sat in one of the chairs on the lawn, still wearing her print uniform dress and belt, sipping a dry sherry which her father had poured for her.

'Supper is almost ready,' her mother said. 'Fresh salmon tonight. You like that, don't you, Anna?'

'Who wouldn't. We don't have it often, Mum.'

'We eat a lot of fish, naturally. Which brings us to something we want to talk to you about.'

'Oh! I should go and change.'

'Later.' Her father, who had been studying her, said quietly. 'Aren't you due for a holiday soon, Annabel? You certainly look in need of one . . .'

'Yes,' she said honestly. 'I feel like one, Dad. It's coming up soon. End of next month, actually. I just want to stay here and laze around and read some books and just please myself generally. Lovely thought . . .'

'Oh . . . Well, your mother and I have a proposition to make . . .'

Eve had broken in then. 'Darling—we want you to come over to Iceland for a couple of weeks. Don't worry about finance—we'll book your flight and send you the tickets if we know the date. It's a complete break you need—lots to show you too . . .'

'And we shan't rush you around,' her father put in before she could speak, 'unless you want to tour round a bit. See the country. Reykjavik is a lively town anyway. There's plenty to do if you want to. Climate is good about now, and we do have a goodish garden, though not like this, of course.'

'Iceland . . .' she said. 'I can't imagine it. But you don't have to pay for my holiday, Dad. I'm not exactly a spendthrift, you know.'

'Neither do you have too big a salary to be able to be one. We want you to come. We'll enjoy showing you around and—having you to ourselves for a time. Will you come?'

'I'd love to, Dad. Thanks.' She kissed him impulsively. How exciting to have it to look forward to. 'But . . .' her face fell, 'What about Gran? I can't be away . . .'

'I . . .' Jane said tranquilly, 'will be staying with Maude. I'm just waiting to get the dates confirmed, and then she and Laurence will drive down, stay the night and take me back to the Cotswolds next day.'

'You've all been talking about me,' Anna protested.

'That's right,' her grandmother agreed amid laughter. 'You've lost weight and you're pushing yourself a bit with all these early mornings and exhausting days on the wards. You haven't had a day off this week either.'

'Oh, dear. Isn't she a sergeant major?' Anna observed, smiling affectionately at her, 'but a real holiday would be nice, I admit. Something to plan for. What clothes would I need?'

With her parents gone back and Tim away most of the time, her life was regimented once more. Having been assigned to Rowan or Regis Ward on a more permanent basis, she knew what her duties were to be and enjoyed going to the hospital each day. Sister was away on holiday and as long as Anna could manage on Rowan, she was expected to do so, calling on a Sister from the other wards only if and when it was necessary.

So she was inevitably working with Dr Lancing and the two registrars.

That morning, Mr Lonsdale was making his round, followed by the usual retinue of Dr Keslar, Dr Grant and Dr Lancing, Anna and three nurses, including the male nurse, when she could get him allocated to Rowan. Two students made up the rear.

As she was standing-in for Sister, she was naturally included in all Mr Lonsdale's comments and directions. When they came to Robert's bed, and watched his anxious face, sharing his anxiety, for he had been re-admitted and undergone a second operation. Mr Lonsdale read through his notes and smiled as he approached his bed.

'I think we've beaten it this time, Robert. Good news, isn't it? You can go home day after tomorrow. Come and see me in outpatients in two weeks. Make a note of that, Staff. It's extremely unlikely that this will occur again, but you'll have to take it quietly for a month or two you know. Be sensible about it.' He put a hand reassuringly on the blue-towelled shoulder, before going on to his next patient.

'Thank you, Sir,' Robert called after him, 'for everything you've done for me.'

Mr Lonsdale accepted his thanks with a gentle nod. He was used to hearing those words now, but they still made it all worthwhile. There were other times when he had to say, 'I'm so very sorry. There is nothing more I can do . . .' and never did he utter those words without suffering a little himself.

This time, when Robert's eyes found hers among the crowd of medics, and he showed his great relief with a 'thumbs up' sign, she stepped back unthinkingly, sharing it with him, right into Dr Keslar, immediately behind her. His arms steadied her at once, his hand on her bare arm, firm. Mr Lonsdale appeared to notice nothing, walking on ahead, but Paul saw the blush which coloured her face; so did the rest of the patients as she heard later. But just now, they were overcome by the hushed atmosphere which prevailed during the consultant's round. But immediately he left the ward, the buzz began and those who could were already on the move in their wheelchairs, or on foot, exchanging his remarks to them avidly. It was all they had to make the time pass, after all.

One evening, Anna left the ward early. For once, there was a full staff and Sister told her to take the opportunity and get off to catch her bus, because her car was at the garage for servicing.

'Oh, thanks, Sister. I'll do the same for you some-time. The buses are so infrequent in the evenings.'

'Go then, while you can . . .' she was told good-humouredly. 'Tomorrow, it may be my turn.'

She hadn't realised it was such a warm evening, because the ward had seemed pleasantly cool; but as she walked towards the main gate, off came her navy cardigan and she wished she wasn't wearing the re-gulation black shoes. They did absolutely nothing for one. She refused to let the fact that she hadn't her car waiting make her frustrated and vexed. Nevertheless, she made no attempt to hide her delight when the green Citroen pulled up beside her and Paul leaned across to open the door for her.

'No car, Staff Nurse? How fortunate I'm a few minutes later tonight.'

'Oh yes . . . I couldn't believe my luck when you stopped at the gate. Just to the bus station will be fine. I think there's one out at a quarter to . . .'

He gave her a wicked grin as he changed gear. 'I'm naturally taking you all the way, Anna; and there's nothing you can do about it.'

'I have no intention of trying . . .' she said happily, as she fastened her seat belt, 'even though it is out of your way.'

'Why didn't you give me a buzz? I'd have waited. I could have missed you.'

'I—thought you had gone,' she told him frankly. 'I saw Mr Lonsdale drive off at five.'

'Had a couple of late patients,' he conceded, 'and Dr Lancing is off at the weekend for her holiday. There were a few ends to tie up. When do you take yours?'

She told him about her parents' proposal and that she would be flying out at the end of August.

'They're quite right. You do need a break. And away from home.'

He turned to give her a brief glance before turning into the lane leading up to the Oast House. It wound for almost two miles, then at the last bend, he braked, slowing down behind a tractor loaded with bales of hay.

'I can't see who's driving it,' he commented. 'Would it be your farmer?'

'I shouldn't think so. Maybe one of his brothers. I saw Mervyn out in the field we just passed. And— he isn't my farmer, you know.'

Something in her voice made him say seriously,

'Is that definite, Anna. I had the impression that you and he had something going in quite a big way.'

'Then you were wrong. He's a specially nice type—they all are. But we're just neighbours. That's all.'

'So Erika was right . . .'

'In what way? Surely you weren't discussing me.' She bridled her voice, taking on a cool note as he crept up behind the wobbling hay, putting a hand quickly over hers in her lap.

'Don't be angry. There's no need. It was just something I said on our way home that night when we came over.'

'I'm surprised you were that interested,' she began, aware that it sounded childish.

'You aren't surprised at all, Anna, but I get the feeling that I'm on dangerous ground, so perhaps we should talk about something less personal. Isn't that the Oast House? I turn in here somewhere, don't I?'

'The white gate on the right.'

She was at the same time relieved and yet sorry that the intimacy of being alone in the car had to end. She would have liked it to go on just a little longer, aware that something was bubbling just under the surface which she wasn't sure about and dare not surmise; she just could be wrong.

Gran was delighted to see Paul, making no secret of it. At her age she didn't have to be circumspect. But it was Anna who asked tentatively if he would like to stay to supper.

He looked down at her, her soft hair shining in the gold of the evening sun, before he said enthusiastically, 'I'd love to—but are you sure? I'm rather taking advantage of your generosity. This is the second time—I can't possibly refuse, Anna.'

'Then don't,' she smiled disarmingly. 'It's only cold, I'm afraid, but you're very welcome. After all, you did come out of your way to bring me home.'

'I know ...' his eyes were laughing before his mouth broke into a smile, 'and I couldn't have arranged it better, obviously.'

'Come on in then and have a sherry or something with Gran while I dash upstairs and change. I smell of Savlon. Even Shane disowns me.'

When she came down, wearing a green silk shirt and slacks, he was sitting, looking quite at home, one long leg crossed over his knee, on the cream linen-covered settee. He sipped his cold beer, which he had preferred to sherry, and watched her descend the curving iron of the stairs. Gran also looked up. She had thoroughly enjoyed her few minutes entertaining him by herself.

Anna, going straight into the kitchen, saw that Gran had an apple pie browning already in the oven. She deftly mixed the green salad and put on some soup to heat and ground coffee beans.

Over supper, the conversation turned to Iceland, of her father's impressions after having lived there for almost a year and her own proposed visit in a few weeks.

'Have you ever been to Iceland, Paul?' Gran asked innocently.

'Not yet, Mrs Forster.' Anna was sure she caught a hint of amusement, however tolerant, in the face he lifted from his meal, but it was gone as he turned back to the salad on his side plate.

She was thinking how natural it seemed to have him there at their table when she noticed that a little of the reserve she associated with him had crept in, although he was still very appreciative. Perhaps he would always hold something of himself in this kind of reserve, she thought. Some part of him where no-one would ever trespass. When one would never quite know what his thoughts were, or why he had gone silent. Being a truthful, outgoing person herself it never occurred to her to tread warily. Unless it was forced upon her, or she had suffered a hurt.

But during the next two hours she learned a great deal more about him. At no time did he mention the hospital. Neither did she. It was more an exchange of views, comments and quite a lot about holidays.

His were now spent in Wales with his father. 'I used to like camping—places like the South of France—then twice I got as far as Sicily—Crete, but latterly, I've been quite happy to stay nearer home. You'll be flying over, Anna, of course.'

'Oh, yes. It's quite a short journey. A couple of hours, I should think.'

'And you'll be staying in Reykjavik, the capital?'

'Just on the outskirts, actually. My parents have

rented a house and although it's a little austere it's quite charming, as are all the friends they've made there. Naturally they miss being here, but it's only temporary and, of course, my father is revelling in the research they're doing on the comparatively unknown part of the Westman Islands.

'Oh—the eruption—six or seven years ago.'

'Yes. Geologically Iceland is terribly exciting for someone like Dad. Rugged and still eruptive, of course. I love mountains and glaciers; anywhere still unspoiled. I like it here too.'

'You'd like Wales . . .' he said.

'I have been there. But only the southern tip. Are you planning a holiday this summer?'

'As I said, only to Wales, I think. No real plans.'

He was looking from the window at the fields and orchards stretching away to the sloping hills, a coffee cup in his hand. She wondered what could be making him look so lost in thought as she started clearing the table while Gran put things away. She had turned on some stereo music softly in the background, and was surprised when he too came into the kitchen and began to dry the dishes.

'Oh—no . . .' she protested. 'We never allow our guests to help with the washing-up.'

'Well—it occurred to me that if I helped—you just might show me the woods, and I saw a stile down the lane leading to a footpath. Does it have a way back again? I haven't climbed a stile since I was at school. Or—are you too exhausted?'

'No. I always take Shane for a run after supper anyway. I'd—like to show you the woods.'

Her heart had leapt excitedly at his suggestion. Did he really think she could miss an opportunity to be with him, away from prying eyes; hear what he had to say to her with only the trees and wood animals to hear?

They had forgotten Gran who was folding away the tablecloth and wouldn't have dreamed of interrupting them, other than to suggest that she finish the dishes while they took advantage of the sunshine; fast going down behind the tall chestnuts flanking the lane. She waived their protests, watching them go, side by side, Shane prancing along in front, with great satisfaction.

Anna was happy. It showed in her light step, in her enthusiasm as they crossed over the lane and into the golden lit shadows under the trees. She stopped, her face like a child, listening.

'Can you hear it?'

He was watching her face, obediently still.

'What am I listening for? I can't hear anything.'

'That's it. The quiet. Isn't it heaven?'

Looking up at him for confirmation, the delighted wonder still in her half smile, in the clear eyes so confident in her own environment, wanting to share it with him, she realised that, although he was quietly amused, there was something deeper. She caught her breath, a little unsure now, afraid to trust what she thought she saw in his eyes directly looking into hers as if he too was unable to believe what he saw in hers. He took an involuntary step, cracking a twig beneath his foot, his hand gripping her arm, hers already reaching for him. So they came together, their bodies touching, his arms holding her fiercely, his cheek against hers; his heart was beating just as fast as her own. She could hear it thudding as they clung together.

'Oh—Anna—how I've wanted to do this.'

She reached to meet his lips with her own, felt the

passion fire his body as if with an electric current, while they kissed, gently, naturally, searchingly, then hers were parting as new feelings were unleashed, surging through her, and her hands touching now the back of his head which had always seemed so untouchable, curled into his hair as she revelled in the strength of his arms. Then, running his fingers gently over her face, her hair, murmuring, 'My lovely Anna . . .' they drew apart at last, looking deeply, almost unbelievingly into each other's eyes, reading the truth there while happiness spread like the morning sun over the fields.

'I love you, Anna.' There was a husky note in this voice, usually so firm and precise. 'To me you are the loveliest, most natural woman I have ever known. Your marvellous skin, your hair—the way you walk; and those expressive eyes—do you know what you've been doing to me ever since I came to the Royal?'

'How could I know?' she teased. 'You were so cross those first two days. I thought I'd done something you didn't like.'

'I didn't want to get involved with anything remotely emotional,' he told her honestly. 'For reasons I won't go into now. And yet, the moment I turned into that corridor and saw you, I knew that I had been waiting for someone like you. You blush like a rose. It reminds me every time of one which grew near the gate in Wales. You really got to me. I hated to admit it and it was hell seeing you with Farmer Abbot that night. Then Erika said you had told her and Sister that you weren't seriously going out with him.'

'Oh, Paul . . .' she was half laughing, yet there were tears in her eyes as she told him how she had felt on that first morning and every day since.

'I thought you and Dr Lancing—how could I know that you felt as I did?' she finished shyly, looking down at their hands holding fast to the other.

'Shall we walk a little?'

She nodded, feeling a tremor of sheer delight when his arms slid round her shoulders and her hair, just under his chin, was pressed by his lips.

Shane, coming back to see what all the delay was about, turned and rushed ahead again, but there were several times when Anna and Paul stopped beneath a sheltering tree and how easily her lips were raised to his. She knew now how Paul, the reserved doctor and man, could just as quickly lose that reserve. He would be a marvellous lover when that time came, as it would, very soon now, and her blush was back, throbbingly so.

They sat close together on the stile, watching the last pink glow disappear and darkness descend on the surrounding countryside. She stirred against him; he got down and lifted her so that she slid down his muscular body. They were part of each other then.

'I want you, Anna,' he told her softly against her ear, so that she too lost control for a moment, then she said with soft certainty, 'And I want you too, Paul. I love you—so very much.'

'My darling Anna. I'm more than ten years older than you are.'

'What does that matter? Not at all. I know you're the only man I have ever felt the least desire to be with for the rest of my life. I'm only happy when I'm with you. We both know how we feel. Nothing else matters, does it?'

'Nothing. Right at this moment, but this . . .' he said softly, kissing her deeply and lengthily once more.

Gran, seeing two figures closely entwined in the gateway, under a watery moon, a few minutes later, tactfully disappeared into her own flat, not even switching on the outside light for them.

Later, after Paul had driven away, she half expected Anna to come to her, but just for tonight, she wanted to keep her new joy secret and intact, besides, it was really too late to disturb Gran. She wanted to relive every moment with Paul, every word. And when at last she slept, the alarm already set for six o'clock, there was a smile on her curved lips and she awoke to the birds chattering outside her window and an extraordinary lightness of heart.

CHAPTER SIX

THERE was something specially uplifting as she went out into the early morning with the dew still wet and scintillating on the grass and baby rabbits, white tails bobbing, sought the comparative safety of their burrows when Shane bounded towards them. The sun was already so bright, it seemed to give everything a new dimension, unless it was because today she was seeing things differently. She and Paul. It was unbelievably true. His kisses last night—her own natural uninhibited responses, matching his passion with her own awakened self; unbelievably wonderful, to remember his whispered words, the touch of the hands she had watched so many times before, only now they were reaching out to her. Every touch had been devastating—sheer heaven; a barrier crossed. He was no longer the unapproachable, slightly withdrawn doctor, in a disappearing white coat, or just sitting, listening and seeing, behind his desk, or beside her, probing and thinking as he examined a patient or, as she mostly thought of him, going from her at the end of the day, out of sight, out of reach, to his own world.

Last night he had been the man who held her close, her face against his skin. She called Shane and set off down through the silvery grass in the hollow where they had walked together a few hours earlier. It was darker among the trees, except where the sun filtered through, where she walked and re-lived their exciting hours when she knew he loved her too, until, glancing at her watch, she was brought swiftly back to the more mundane demands of the present. How could she have forgotten that her car was at the garage and she was going to have to walk to the bus stop?

Back at the house she tugged off her rubber boots in the porch, surprised to see her grandmother, still wearing her house coat, in the doorway.

'Didn't you hear the phone, Anna?'

'No. I've only just got back. Haven't had any breakfast yet and now there's no time. I have to walk . . .'

'You're being called for at eight o'clock. If you could be out by the gate. That was Paul.'

'Oh—really?'

'So you do have time for breakfast. In fact, I've already started it.'

'Oh—Gran. Thanks. I quite forgot I don't have the car today. I'm so used to just getting in and taking off, I suppose.'

'Well—forgetting things is not always the perogative of the elderly, you know. I dare say there were other more exciting things on your mind.'

'You're fishing,' Anna said, pouring coffee into her cup without looking up.

'I know. Disgraceful, isn't it? But I can see that you aren't going to tell me so I'll have to be patient a little longer obviously. But there's no mistaking the way your eyes sparkled just now when I said his name. I wasn't born yesterday, you know. I've been in love too, and I remember it all very well. Especially in the beginning.'

'I'm afraid to believe it yet, Gran. I'm so happy, it isn't true. To be so much in love and know that Paul feels the same way about me.'

'Yes. It is wonderful,' Jane said softly. 'Cherish it, Anna. I am so happy for you both. Paul is right for you. Your parents are going to be delighted. But I must get myself dressed. He'll be here soon. There's more toast in the toaster. I wonder if he's had breakfast.'

'I'm sure he has,' Anna said laughingly, 'and I'm beginning to suspect that I have competition . . .'

'If I was forty years younger you certainly would have,' Gran called back over a retreating shoulder. 'I think he's a lovely man.'

'I think so too,' Anna told herself as she ran up the curving stairs to her room and hastily made her bed, leaving everything tidy before going down to wait for Paul.

When his car slid to a standstill at the gate, she got in quickly so that she wouldn't waste his time, or her own, and waited for his kiss, but he simply said, as the car shot forward, 'You look crisp and cool this morning. How are you?'

She murmured with raised eyebrows, 'You make me feel like one of your patients. I'm fine, thank you.'

She saw his face relax into a half smile, but he didn't speak, taking the bends in the lane skilfully, looking every inch the surgeon this morning in conventional grey suit and grey and white striped shirt with a dark red tie. Even his hair fell neatly into place over the wide forehead. Last night she had seen it ruffled, like a small boy after a football game. Today he was a little out of reach and a feeling of latent disappointment slowly crept through her body.

Could she be imagining that he had switched off and all the happenings of last evening had been deliberately lost, somewhere in the night hours?

Tremendous pride kept her from asking. He probably had more serious things on his mind this morning. Besides, she was used to remaining silent unless it was necessary to direct any remarks to her surgeons as part of her working day, so she was able to more easily control the words trembling on her lips than most girls would have been, respecting his need for no chat. Instead, she contented herself by watching his hands on the wheel. Strong, yet sensitive hands; with well-shaped nails. She wanted to touch them, feel his fingers close convulsively around her own, as they had yesterday. She looked down at them now, folded in her lap. Unlike his, they were subjected to too much water, hardened with disinfecting agents; even gardening when she forgot to put on her gloves.

'Heavens—this lane is never-ending, isn't it? Wonder why it has so many bends—couldn't they have straightened it a little? You must find it extremely hazardous sometimes. There's no way of knowing if something is around the corner and it's so narrow in parts.'

'I know why it twists the way it does. There's a simple explanation which I found in one of the local magazines. It's because the road was cut through the forest and had to be made this way to avoid the trees. The monks are said to have used it on their way to the monastery.'

'Ah . . .' He turned to chuckle at her and the air suddenly cleared and her spirits rose. 'Such a simple explanation—as you say. I ought to have guessed that my practical girl would know the answer.'

'I'm practical—because I have to be.' She bridled as he went on.

'I know. But you have a great many other assets

too, which I also admire.' His voice softened. 'You're caring and sensitive, Anna. Gentle, as a woman should be, yet strong when you need to be. Intelligent. A girl of whom any man would be proud. Oh—much more. It's going to be very exciting to discover them, one by one, I think.'

'Oh, Paul . . .' She could barely speak for the emotion gathering in her throat. Impulsively, she slid her hand under his arm, feeling the muscles tense under his jacket.

Soon the hospital walls came into sight and she withdrew her hand as they drove in through the gates and he stopped in the space reserved for the doctors.

'Will your car be ready today?'

She nodded. 'This afternoon. They're bringing it here for me.'

'Oh, fine. I'm tied up this evening, I'm afraid. It looks like being a long day, but—one gets used to those.'

'Oh . . .' she said contritely, 'I'm to blame for your earlier than usual start.'

'Not at all. Don't look so pensive. I want to kiss you but I don't intend to give anyone the opportunity to discuss our personal life. You wouldn't want that either, so we had better start protecting it. Have a good day.'

'You too.' He leaned over to open her door. She caught the faint smell of his cologne which she now associated with his masculinity and which she thought was Monsieur Givenchy, having chosen the same soap for her father's Christmas present last year. It was extremely hard not to touch his face with her lips—so close. But she knew she must desist and it was only later that she remembered the moment again and wondered at her own impulsiveness. After all, only last night it would have been completely natural—he would have wanted it too; probably crushed her to him, there under the trees; yet today, it was quite out of context.

She had gone into the building through a separate door from Paul, joining up with Jill Slade along the corridor to the changing rooms.

'Did I see you in Dr Keslar's car just now?' she asked bluntly.

'You know you did.'

'Where did he pick you up then?'

'Oh, along the way. My car is in for a service.'

'Oh, I see. He's in early, isn't he? Perhaps he's got an early appointment. Is he operating this morning?'

'Yes.'

'I wanted to ask you what you think about my going over to the chest hospital if there's a vacancy this autumn. I can't quite make up my mind, but I do honestly want a change, Anna. I've had it up to here in O.P.'

'What's brought this on, Jill? You're serious, aren't you?'

'Deadly. I think one of the reasons is transport. I can't face another winter standing around waiting for buses and I'd be hopeless at driving. The Chest Annexe is much closer to home and it would be pointless to move when I've got everything I want there. Besides—my mother needs all the help I can give just now. There are problems . . .'

'Oh—I'm sorry. In that case, why don't you have a word with the P.N.O.? I know they could do with more higher grade nurses over there. But then, we can too.'

'Especially down in O.P. Auxiliaries, yes; but experienced nurses are a bit thin on the ground. I really don't know . . .'

'Come on, cheer up. Not one of your best days, Jilly. And it's going to be such a lovely one outside. There isn't a cloud in the sky.'

'I know. They're all in here. Imagine being shut inside these walls doing the same things all day. Perhaps that's it. I need a bit more challenge.'

'I think . . .' Anna said carefully, 'that you do need to think seriously about a change of direction, Jill. Do something about it, love.'

'Which means making an appointment to see Miss Parkinson sometime today. Thanks.'

'Right. And I'm due on Rowan in exactly three minutes. Let me know how you make out, won't you?'

Not waiting for the lift, Anna ran lightly up the grey stone stairs, arriving on the ward looking as fresh as the morning outside the windows, and her smile as the doors swung behind her matched the soft glow about her skin and eyes which was positively infectious. More than one pyjama-clad man was infused with something akin to hope and even a stirring of his senses as she greeted them on her way to the table which served as a desk.

'Aye . . .' she heard George Bray remark under his breath, as he thought, to his neighbour, 'she's a real tonic, that girl. We've a lot to be thankful for when the young nurses keep coming like her.'

And that from a man with a recently amputated leg. It made her feel suddenly very humble, cutting one down to size, she decided as she picked up the report sheet and had a quick word with the staff nurse who had been on night duty.

Sister had a meeting at ten, so there was a great deal of reorganising to do, and Anna, working her way through the morning, delegating tasks and responsibilities, arranging for the patients who were going to theatre to be prepared and monitored and accompanied, no slip ups, was motivated by the inner happiness which stemmed from her love for Paul.

Yet somewhere, right at the back of her consciousness, there was a tiny niggle, unrecognised yet and certainly undefined, mainly because she didn't want to bring it out in the open yet. She wanted nothing to mar the joy of discovering their love for each other. Because she loved Paul so much, sometimes it hurt, physically.

But alone in the kitchen, carefully measuring out milk for the patients' elevenses, her wayward thought finally surfaced. She knew what was really bugging her. She had been simply expecting that Paul would greet her this morning in the same vein as his last words to her a few hours before. Instead, he had stressed the need for secrecy about their feelings for each other. Why? Unless it would bring some embarrassment to either of them. Which she knew could happen. So what had she expected? That he would want to announce an engagement or something equally definite? How naive can one get? Premature even. He hadn't said anything about sharing a future together, had he? She had simply taken it for granted. Because it was so special, so obviously real for her; did it have to be for him? Her face flared as she remembered what she had said when they sat close together on that stile, after he murmured that he was ten years her senior. 'You're the only man I've ever felt the least desire to be with for the rest of my life,' she had told him. 'Nothing else matters, does it?'

'Nothing.' He meant it. She was sure. Hadn't he followed it up with that kiss which seemed to submerge her physically and mentally? When they seemed a part of each other's emotions. Was he holding back today? Regretting anything? Or was she just too imaginative because today his professional world had first claim?

Jolting her mind to the task she was immediately engaged upon, she resolutely pushed everything else to the back of her mind. It was much too soon to be setting the pace anyway. Of course she knew that. Paul had said he loved her. She didn't imagine he would say it lightly. He wasn't the type. It should be enough.

The door swung open and Sister, bustling in with a query and a worried frown, gave her the impetus needed to bring her thoughts into final perspective. There was not an unoccupied minute after that. One of the patients, returning to the ward after a gall-bladder removal, needed constant surveillance, but she was ordered away for her two hours' off-duty by Sister just the same, and when she returned, Paul and Dr Lancing were at the bedside and the oxygen cylinder was in place.

Her heart literally turned over it seemed when Paul straightened up and thoughtfully looked down at his patient before saying something to Dr Lancing. He's so caring, she thought tenderly. He won't go until he's assured that Mrs Priory is okay.

Sister had gone. Anna sat at her desk filling in reports, looking up again a moment later. Paul too was writing something. The back of his head, showing the clean, dark line of his hair, shoulders forward;

his image under the white coat dear to her now. He loved her—Anna Forster. Wasn't that enough? She hugged her precious secret to herself. It was enough. Of course he had been perfectly right to want to keep their personal life apart from the hospital one.

He was coming with purposeful steps towards her table. She stood up. Their eyes found each other's and there was an immediate impact, but only for a moment before his were veiled, serious again. She too was now outwardly controlled, aware of the house doctor's interest also as she waited for him.

He spoke quickly, outlining the problem and explaining the extra medication he wanted given to her.

'Dr Lancing will be around,' he ended, 'should she be needed. I have to be in two places at once in just over half an hour.'

'I see. Thank you Dr Keslar.' She was already writing in Mrs Priory's notes as the doctors went out of sight.

When she looked down from the window an hour later she saw that her small car was sitting out there on the tarmac as promised. It gave her a return of the independence she preferred. On her way she stopped to speak to a new patient who was getting used to the feel of the hard hospital bed and felt shy, because everyone around her was a stranger.

'Not for long,' Anna assured her, pushing up the tall window to let in the soft, summer breeze. Somewhere down among the rooftops in the ancient town, a clock struck five. Everyone was closing their offices, shops; the day almost over for them. Two hours longer for her, and several small necessary things to be done yet. But given the choice, no way would she change her job.

Dr Lancing came in then, slumping into a chair at Sister's table, putting down the report notes in the folder she carried.

'Mrs Jones's notes . . .' she said, in a clipped voice. 'There was nothing Mr Lonsdale could do. So she's been sutured—and that's that. Hopelessly advanced—far worse than he suspected. It didn't show too much on the X-rays but—there it is.'

'Oh—I *am* sorry.' Anna groaned with real feeling.

'So . . .' Erika let out a long sigh and got to her feet. 'Will you ask, or leave a message, for Mr Jones when he comes in tonight, to see me? I'll be around . . .'

'Of course.'

She watched for a moment the doctor who seemed to have lost all her off-duty charm, but none of her dignity, as she walked heavily from the ward, and not for the first time Anna registered that the medical profession had to be the most draining of them all.

She couldn't easily shake off her more serious mood as she drove home that evening. Apart from the fights and setbacks where the patients were involved, there was still the latent disappointment of her conversation with Paul. Surely he could have shown in some way that he hadn't forgotten everything. She had thought that it would all be so different today, yet it wasn't. She had felt secure emotionally last night. But today—was quite the opposite.

Her expression was still subdued, unlike her normal one, because the corners of her mouth were naturally turned up and not like now, droopy, as she brought her car to a standstill. When Shane bounded towards her, she absently bent to rub his ears before going into the kitchen to pour herself a dry Martini, exclaiming with annoyance when the ice-cubes cascaded from the tray over the table.

Gran came from her room when she heard Shane's bark of welcome and after one glance at Anna's face, wisely said nothing as she helped gather them up. But a few moments later she said quietly, as she busied herself with their meal, 'What is it, dear? A bad day?' Even more concerned when her granddaughter said crossly, 'What's what?' as she sat down and kicked off her shoes. 'I'm sorry, Gran . . .' emerged after Anna had watched her cutting up mushrooms for an omelette over the top of her glass for a few seconds. 'Actually, there's no reason; just me. It's been an odd kind of day. I feel a bit out of my depth, I suppose.'

'That's not like you.'

'I know. You see—I should be on top of the world. Well, I was, but somehow it seems to have evaporated. Oh, well—that's life. One minute on cloud nine, the next, down in the valley.'

'Do you want to tell me about it or not? It's Paul, isn't it?'

'How did you know?'

Two delicately shaped eyebrows were raised as she regarded Anna with some amusement. 'My dear girl, I'm not blind. I had hoped you were going to tell me that you and he were in love. Obviously not.'

'But we are . . .' It was out before Anna could think. Her eyes softened then sparkled as rapturous moments were re-lived. 'It's so incredible, Gran; that it's me . . .'

'I don't think there's anything incredible about

that. You're so right for each other, and I think he's got a bargain. He was attracted to you from the start, anyone could see that, and I'm so happy for you. It's wonderful news, dear. But why so despondent for heaven's sake? Is there a problem?'

'No. Of course not. You see—we haven't been able to talk to each other much today and it only happened last night.'

'Your parents will be delighted.'

'I won't tell them for a day or two . . .'

'Are you engaged or not?'

'Not, I would say.'

'Oh—well—Paul must feel very deeply about you, because when we were talking about his father in Wales, he explained, even stressed, that he didn't plan to marry or put down roots anywhere for years yet, for several reasons.'

'Did—did he say what they were, Gran?' Anna's voice seemed to have got lost in her throat.

'Mainly his commitment towards his father, I think. He maintains the house in Wales I gather, because it was the family home and he, Dad that is, seems happy there. There is a housekeeper and a resident nurse and a man to look after the garden, which, besides having a small flat of his own, can't be easy. He is a very dedicated young man, Anna, and planned to achieve consultancy level before thinking of a home and family of his own. Obviously, my grand-daughter has made him change his mind.'

'I—don't think so,' Anna said as she got up and went upstairs to her room. She was absorbing what she had just heard, though why he should open up to Jane, she didn't know, except that they liked each other and were able to converse easily, possibly because of her age.

Now, a prickly sensation was erupting and gathering momentum as it sped through the nerves of her body. Paul hadn't said one word to make her think his plans involved any permanency in their relationship. Simply that he loved her. She knew how much he wanted her, as she wanted him. They were adult people. She longed for him now; ached for his arms, his touch, reassurance that last night was real for him too. As she stared at her flushed cheeks in the mirror, she knew that if Paul wanted it that way, so did she. Nothing could come between them; it was too deep. Disturbingly compelling—this new emotion he had created—did he realise that? It was throwing her off balance, just a bit, because it was the first time it had happened and she didn't yet know herself under the image most other people saw from the outside.

Changing into slacks and a cotton top, she made her way into the woods with Shane. It was the only place she could regain some semblance of her normally clear-thinking self.

Later, as she dug in the borders around the house, she felt she had achieved something aimed for and it was almost dark, the mosquitos bothersome, when she went inside the house and upstairs for her bath.

She was looking for a book to read in bed when the phone extension in her room bleeped. Her mother perhaps, she thought, as she picked it up, her mind running on the proposed visit to Iceland.

'Anna . . .' She caught the intimate inflexion in his voice.

'It's you . . .' Her heartbeats doubled.

'I thought you might be asleep. I've just got back. You seem so out of reach today, I had to convince myself that—you aren't. What are you doing?'

'Sitting on the side of my bed after my bath, feeling so happy now that I can hear your voice,' she answered honestly.

'Oh—my darling. This is the part of the day when I need you. I've had to ruthlessly shut you out of my thoughts all day—you have a habit of projecting your image, your eyes—those expressive eyes—right before me at the wrong time. As at tonight's lecture—just because I caught sight of a medical student in the third row with hair the colour of yours— and that won't do. We have to do something about us, my Annabel ... I'm a man in love as never before—and it's not going to go away, you adorable girl.'

She was between tears and laughter now.

'Paul—I'm so glad. You see, I thought you didn't—and you do. Please—never stop loving me this way. I've discovered that I'm such a romantic at heart, but I didn't think you were too. I think I understand now. Thank you for calling me.'

'Then sleep on it, Anna. See you tomorrow. Goodnight, darling.'

'Goodnight,' she echoed, with stars in her eyes and happiness flooding her whole body.

'Paul phoned last night,' she told Jane at breakfast, assuming a nonchalant air.

'I'm so glad. I expect you slept well after that. You look very bright this morning.'

Anna smiled dreamily. 'I feel absolutely fine,' she said. 'It's going to be hot again. I think I'll wear a cotton dress and change at the hospital.'

Paul saw her getting out of her car as he turned in through the gates. Her soft cotton dress caught the morning breeze and as she walked, head high, her cream sandals and shoulder bag matching the yellow of her dress, he thought she was the most feminine, the most perfect woman he had known in his life until then. And she was his lovely Anna. There was no question, no doubt anywhere. He wanted her for his wife. If only it was that simple.

He sat watching her, enjoying the picture she made, until she disappeared in through the door and along the white-tiled corridor.

Then he reached for his black briefcase and, after locking his car, followed more leisurely, going in through another entrance. He was deliberately early this morning. He wanted to catch up on some notes, also to read through the case-book of a patient on Rowan who was something of a problem and so far neither he nor Mr Lonsdale had come up with any answer in spite of all the usual tests.

Meanwhile, Anna had changed and was exchanging a few words with Margo, now in Theatre, but on Rowan when she had first come to the Royal.

'Have you seen our new consultant anaesthetist, Dr Eyre?' she asked as she pinned on her cap. 'Oh— this wretchedly silly thing—it's all got to come off again when I get into theatre—but I just might meet the P.N.O. along one of the corridors. Be just my luck. Yes—he's got the most bewitching moustache, Anna. It turns up at the ends and when he's got his green cap on, he looks gorgeous. Besides that, he's really nice, not giving away anything—not an inch, though he doesn't have to say anything—you just know if there's something—and you take darned good care then there isn't. It's great in theatre now, mind you, I still miss the ward. You're still on Rowan, aren't you?'

Anna nodded, going towards the door. 'Coming?'

'Not quite ready. See you around.'

'Yes. And I have met Dr Eyre. He's everything you say.' She was happy in the knowledge that Dr Paul Keslar would be taking outpatients all day, probably until five tonight; maybe—just maybe—he would come up to the ward, but it was probably better for her peace of mind, also her concentration, if he did not. And today there was nothing to mar the smile which was normally there as she went from one bed to the next, finding out how each patient was this morning, recognising a woman who had been re-admitted during the night and now looked very much like having surgery to remove the gall-stones which had given her so much trouble before.

Later in the morning, Mr Lonsdale, with Paul at his side, decided to do a cholecystectomy on her, and Sister came to give Anna detailed instructions. And so it went on. But today she could go quietly from one job to the next, with no hint of the inner confusion of yesterday. In the late afternoon there was a lecture she wanted to attend. Right at the end she noticed that Paul had come into the lecture hall and was standing at the back. How odd. What could he possibly learn that he didn't know already? Actually, he simply wanted a word with Dr Roberts.

As she left, he turned and saw her. His mouth twitched as if he was controlling a delighted grin.

'Hullo, Staff Nurse—I'm just coming up to Rowan if you'll wait a second . . .'

'Of course, Dr Keslar.'

She hid the mischief in her eyes quite successfully, standing in the corridor, eyes running down the notes she had made.

Then he was beside her, white coated, very real

and purposeful as he strode along beside her.

'Can we meet tomorrow evening?' He kept his voice deliberately casual. She understood why as several nurses, housemen, even consultants, used this corridor, and they *were* walking side by side.

'I'd like that. Will you come over to the Oast House?'

'I'll collect you at eight. Perhaps you'd like to see where I live—I think we must talk about us, don't you?'

'Yes.' She lowered her eyes. 'I'll be ready, Paul.'

Sister, coming from her office, saw nothing unusual in the fact that he held the door for Anna and touched her shoulder as she went into the ward, before standing back for herself. But to the girl who loved him quite desperately, his touch was sheer magic and her face was pink—with a becoming blush which she couldn't hide—and that was noticed and mentally recorded as Sister, with compressed lips, brought his patients' notes to him by the bed and drew the curtains.

CHAPTER SEVEN

IT was just as well that Paul had no real occasion to visit Rowan Ward the next day, because Anna, not for one moment associating Sister's occasionally quizzical glances with the evening before, would have had no warning to be on her guard. And the light in her eyes would certainly have given her away when he appeared, substantiating the hovering suspicion in Sister's mind that something was definitely going on between her Staff Nurse and the new Senior Registrar, and she did not approve.

But Anna did see him for a fleeting moment as she returned from the dispensary after lunch. He and Dr Lancing were leaving the dining-room together, deeply immersed in conversation. There was a crease on Paul's forehead as he listened.

She was about to turn the corner when a patient back for a routine check, resting on one of the rails, drew her attention.

'It's me, Nurse Forster. You was going right past me. And I never forgot you. You did though . . .'

'Oh—it's Lucy. No—of course not. I just didn't see you.'

'I know. You had eyes for that nice-looking doctor, didn't you? But he's got his lady one . . .'

'How are you now, Lucy?'

'I'm doing all right, love.' She chuckled. 'I really thought I was a gonner this time, didn't I? I guess I might have been if it wasn't for you. Oh—you was good to me. Lucy don't forget.'

'Well, I can't tell you how glad I am to see you looking so well. Keep it up, and take care. I have to rush, Sister's waiting for these. 'Bye Lucy.'

Paul and Erika had gone. As she went upstairs, she thought of the rewards in her profession. Like now, seeing Lucy; who literally gave up after her left leg was amputated, and here she was, walking with a stick and her newly-fitted limb. Anna had been very involved with her, because she had been the only one to break through, using special tactics and a good sprinkling of psychology, preparing her to go back to her one room again and manage for herself.

It was lovely seeing Paul again too. Last night, when he had rung her again, the emotion in his voice had even come across the wires. The way he had said her name. And tonight—there would be just the two of them. In his flat, unobserved and un-interrupted, something so far denied them, except for the time in the woods.

Of course she no longer resented Erika, knowing that their relationship was purely professional, though she did feel a trifle guilty that Erika was unaware that Paul and she were in love. That he wouldn't be taking her out socially any more. She might even wonder why. Anyone could see how much she admired him.

But Sister was waiting and together they checked through the drugs and Paul was dismissed from her mind.

'Mr Lonsdale has asked for tests from Mr Randal, Staff. Get the usual ones done, will you? Dr Lancing will be in later for some blood tests. The Path Lab are on a go slow and we need them.'

'Yes, Sister. Perhaps I'll let Nurse Osman help.

She needs some practical. I think she is very promising.'

'I thought so too. But watch her, for heaven's sake. Check and re-check. You know that, of course. I'm off now . . .'

Anna's practised eyes missed nothing as she walked back through the ward. Some patients slept. Others watched the clock until it was time for the visitors. Others no longer cared. She called the first-year nurse over to the bed. 'Now, these are all routine tests, as you know. Dr Lancing will take some blood tests later, so we're looking for chlorides and cholesterol level now. Oh—I'd better let the visitors in.'

She went out from behind the curtains and the hum of voices immediately grew in the ward and the feet and scraped chairs began. Going back, Anna quickly recognised that the first-year nurse helping her was most promising, gathering up the dressings and clearing away quickly. She had a good manner towards the patients, whether male or female, and was obviously keen to learn.

'Right, Nurse, just draw back the curtains and then make us a cup of tea, will you? Oh—dear! On the way, get Mr Lane back into his pyjama trousers. What does he think he is doing?'

She put her head round the door of the day room to fetch one of the male patients back to his bed to have his dressings changed. In here they mostly watched television or snoozed, finding a brief respite from the pain, even in limbs they no longer had. Amputations were routine ops on Rowan, and the saving of them, an eternal fight for the surgeons and, when it all became too much, Anna's only words to help them in their frustration and pain, were 'Take one day at a time. It will be better tomorrow. You'll cope. They all do. Be brave.' And they all were, because the pain was shared.

It was a long time until she could at last walk out, exhausted mentally and physically, and leave it all behind. But the picture conjured up of her meeting with Paul, the decisive evening ahead, especially when she saw that his car had gone, hours earlier probably, soon took over and she drove home as fast as she dared.

A bath first and, as she dressed, her exhilaration mounted. It would be lovely to see his flat and be able to visualise him there from tonight on. She felt intoxicated with the thought of their being together, yet just a niggle of apprehension too. Was it such an impossible dream? Why did she feel this way? She just couldn't imagine why. Neither was she sure whether she was supposed to eat with him or before he came. So she settled for a chicken sandwich and an apple. Gran was out visiting friends in the town and wouldn't be back until later.

There was a letter from her mother bearing the Icelandic postmark on the table. She read it while her bath was running and now again for the second time while she waited for Paul. Was it really only five weeks to her holiday? Her flight had been booked, her mother wrote, and the tickets would come direct to her. She would have to shop around for new clothes and although she didn't normally go to the summer sales, perhaps this year she should hunt for some reductions. Stedmans, perhaps. But she knew that she didn't want to go away from Paul now, when everything was so promising, so wonderful, not even for two weeks.

And he, turning into the drive just before eight o'clock, saw her with some freshly-cut pink roses which she was putting into a wooden trug, with Shane by her side, and wished he could take the picture with him in more solid form than in his mind.

Putting down the trug, she came to meet him, reaching out with both hands. They went into the house, shoulders touching, saying nothing of consequence until they were inside; and only then did he draw her close to him, strongly, so that his hold was almost intense, their lips merging into a desperate kiss, one which grew longer and deeper until even their heartbeats seemed to merge. At last, they reluctantly parted, and Paul murmured against her hot face:

'I have waited to do that, my darling. Oh—it's so *good* to be with you . . .'

Now it was she who sought his lips. They were ready and waiting and after a few moments when they were both aware of their raised passions, it was she who broke away, shaking her head ruefully. 'Paul—what must you think of me? It's just that— I've longed for you all day, and I'm afraid to let you go, now that you're actually here.'

'We've hours yet . . .' he murmured against her hair. 'And I'll tell you later what I think of you. Are you ready to go?'

She nodded. 'I'll just call Shane. My grandmother is out but she has her key.'

'Good. I'll open up the car.'

They sped along the lanes across country, Anna turning to look back, seeing the Oast House from a new angle behind the hedges bordering the fields. The apples in the orchards were beginning to ripen into colour, shining in the golden rays of the evening sun.

'Oh—I do love living here,' she said.

'Yes. Your father made a very wise choice,' Paul observed, 'especially if this life-style appeals. It is enviable.'

'Does it, to you?'

'I was brought up in the country, so naturally it does.'

'You will probably have a choice one day, where you will settle. If you want to.'

He laughed, then grimaced a little.

'I've not reached that stage yet, Anna. Not to buy a permanent home that is. Although circumstances change. We shall see. But as I've only recently come to Calderbury Royal, I can't see any immediate move for me yet. But—one never knows.'

There was silence in the car. Her mind considering his words. Was he saying that he didn't want any permanency in their relationship? Shouldn't she still tread carefully if she didn't want to have to retract gracefully? Why was she so unsure? She decided to change the course of that particular conversation. So she said lightly,

'I had news from Iceland today. My flight is booked for July thirteenth. Not too long, is it?'

'High season and very expensive, of course. I expect you're looking forward to it.'

'Yes. So are my parents, and they are paying for everything, for which I'm terribly grateful, but . . .'

'But what, darling?'

'I don't think I want to go now.'

'Why?' He threw her a swift, enquiring glance.

'I won't want to be that far away from you,' she said simply.

'Oh . . .' His hand covered hers, lying in her lap, as he told her, 'You really are the most surprising girl and you say the most unexpected, but lovely things. You're so truthful—and I love you. But I have to go to Wales soon, so there have to be separations.'

'I know. Ridiculous, isn't it? One would think it was teenage first love—painful but so real, achingly so. Yet that's exactly how it feels.'

'For me too,' he said quietly, and another swift glance was serious enough to confirm it. 'I haven't given any personal relationships a chance to flourish beyond the initial stages if there was the slightest chance of it becoming out of hand. So this is completely a new experience for me—which may surprise you.'

'It doesn't actually, Paul.'

Then there was no more time.

'Here we are . . .' he said abruptly, turning into a gateway from the lane still outside the village itself, and near to a grey stone church. He drew up in front of a stone house covered with creepers and surrounded with lawns and flower beds.

'Here?' She hadn't expected his flat to be situated in a large house, thinking of it as part of a block. Yet she should have known that in this village there would be nothing like that. Too much out of character. This was a conservation area and every new building carefully chosen to be in keeping.

He came round to open the car door. 'Yes. This is where I live. On the first floor. I think you'll like it. It was the old vicarage, I believe.'

It had obviously been someone's home, she decided, noticing the huge rooms downstairs leading from the hall, its walls and floors seeming to be of oak. She felt a little sad as she followed him up the wide staircase that the house had to be divided up this way, into several apartments, judging by the number of cars outside. It was probably the only means of keeping it going. Paul's name was on a door on the first landing. She waited while he put in his key, then opened it for her to go inside.

She saw at once a table laid for two in the centre of the huge room. 'Have I come to supper?' she asked, turning to him.

'Yes. Surely I said that?'

'No . . .' she said, laughingly. Not for anything was she going to admit to having eaten earlier.

'My cleaning woman prepared it all,' he explained. 'Soup just needs heating and there's a fish pie in the oven. And,' he opened the fridge, 'here is a very attractive fresh fruit salad, made by myself.'

'Really, Paul?'

He nodded delightedly. 'I thought it a good choice for a warm evening.'

'It's lovely—can I do something?'

'No.' She was on the receiving end of a frankly, adoring look as he closed the fridge door and straightened up. 'I like your dress.'

'Thank you,' she smiled back at him, glad that she had chosen her own favourite shirt-waister to wear tonight. She had known instinctively that he liked simple clothes and nothing too fussy. In fact, she was beginning to learn that he had some very definite ideas on some things. He came slowly towards her.

'I like my women to look feminine . . .' he murmured huskily, confirming her choice. 'Besides, you are naturally so, my lovely Anna.'

He kissed her lightly before going to the table and pouring two pale gold sherries into glasses, bringing one to her.

'To us, Anna . . .' he said seriously.

'To us . . .' she echoed.

'Happy?'

'So very happy—it hurts.'

'Darling . . .' he put his glass down and took her in his arms, kissing her this time very expertly, arousing her senses again, so that she had difficulty in breaking away, saying softly, 'I think I can smell the pie.'

'You can . . .' he bounded across to the tiny kitchen and grabbed the oven gloves while she collapsed, helplessly, into the armchair after his exclamation: 'Damn—it's hot . . .'

Then she got up and went to his aid.

'There's a doctor in the house—if you've burned yourself . . .' she said while she took the gloves from him. 'Here—let me. Oh—it's lovely and brown— just in time. The soup too. You're not really burned are you, Paul? If so, put it straight under the cold tap.' At that they broke into helpless laughter because she was unthinkingly prescribing for him.

'Oh—do let's begin,' he said impatiently when calm was restored. 'I'm starving.'

'That's better,' she told him gaily. 'You sound actually human at last.'

'It isn't that bad, is it?'

'Sometimes. At first, I thought you were quite unapproachable until I heard you with one of the patients and realised that you're a terribly caring person actually. Oh, Paul, I had such a complex on that awful day when I dropped everything.'

'I still don't know what was wrong.' He looked up from his soup. 'Did the atmospheric conditions get to you or were you, as I suspected, doing the work of two nurses and had been for quite some time? Also—

I was probably partly at fault because of being in a new habitat and letting it show. I'm sorry about that. But you know, even then, you were having a very recognisable effect on me and that was the last thing I expected to happen or wanted. So—what happened to you? Was it the atmospherics?'

She had finished her soup. 'More than just that. It was the way I felt about you. I was resisting it, I suppose. I couldn't believe I could react so strongly; I was horrified. I had to fight it.'

'Why did you have to?'

'You know why. And I didn't dream you would—love me too,' she ended softly.

'It was the last thing on my mind, Anna. But after three days I couldn't wait to walk through the door and know you would be there. You had a small golden curl on your neck—that first morning . . .'

'Oh, Paul. I had no idea. I'll never really know you, or what you're thinking.'

He came to take her plate. 'You soon will—I promise you.' There was more than a hint of excitation in his voice as he went to fetch the fish pie, declining her help this time very definitely.

Afterwards, when the dishes were stacked and he had made excellent coffee, they carried it back into the other room. He put the tray on the long table in front of the settee and reached for her hand. 'Come and sit down here, Anna. Will you mind if we talk seriously?'

'About us?'

He nodded. 'I'd also like to put you in the picture about my father—my background, if you like, because the hospital isn't quite all of it.'

She had known instinctively that there were problems; that for him it was more complicated than just falling in love and letting the future evolve from there.

'You see—it isn't fair to you, my love—not to know. It hasn't arisen previously; but—I can't let you go, now that I know how very special you've become. How empty it was, before. Except that because of my work, it was probably enough. Because every "spare minute", I've read and studied and attended lectures—and given them. It's been exciting, in its way. One becomes involved. I love what I'm doing; even at the end of the day when one feels literally slammed; that's just all part of it. But then you know all that too. Now I have to re-think. And you're part of that—an inseparable part.'

'What are you trying to tell me, Paul?' Anna asked quietly.

'First, I'd like to tell you about my father and his dependence, to a certain degree, on me—if you like.'

'Financially?'

He nodded. 'There is the house in Wales, which isn't quite paid for—but almost. I am responsible for that now, although I still need another home elsewhere. As you know, he too is, or was, a doctor; a country practitioner, and a popular one at that. He lives outside the village but he had a surgery at the back of the post office to which the whole population seemed to come. That's by the way. Before retirement age he contracted multiple sclerosis. He knew it before I did, naturally.'

'Oh, no . . . I'm so sorry, Paul.'

He went on, speaking as he would to a colleague, in medical terms, and she realised that the degenerating process was well established. That time was running out.

'There are remissions, as you know, but a fall last autumn, in which he sustained a fractured femur, has immobilised him completely. There is permanent paraplegia in both legs. This necessitates having a full-time nurse in the house. She was at the surgery with him for years and is devoted to him. No problems on that score. She also keeps me posted all the time. He hasn't very long now and this does seem the best and only way to help him because he loves his home and the hills all around. I couldn't take any of it away.'

'Why should you have to? Unless of course . . .'

'Oh—with his small income and my contribution—we manage. He also has a housekeeper. She too was one of the villagers. So you see—he is well cared for. But Bronwen rang me last night . . .'

'She is his nurse?'

'Yes. Sorry. I think I should go home either this weekend or next.'

'It must be so much worse when one is aware of every phase of one's illness,' she said sadly. 'Is he able to read?'

'Not much now. And he loved his books. It was one of the compensations to have the time. His study has been turned into his bedroom now. It does simplify things for the two women and he's happier among the things he loves. And there's a wonderful view of the valley from that window.'

She saw that for a moment he had recaptured something which brought nostalgia.

'You love that house and valley too, don't you?'

'Of course. It was where I was born. Where my mother was, my friends. It's home to me. You will feel as I do, Anna. I know that. When can you come and see it with me? I do want you and my father to meet. I told him about you on the phone the other evening. You see—I don't think there is too much time left. Would you like to come with me?' His eyes were expressive.

'Oh—I'd love to, Paul. You must know that. I wonder . . . You see, it's Sister's weekend coming up, and my forty-eight the following week—I'd need longer though, wouldn't I?'

'Well—I hope to be away on Friday afternoon and drive back later on Sunday. It will take around four hours—if we're lucky. The new motorway helps, of course.'

'I'll ask her tomorrow.'

'But—will you have to explain why you need longer?'

'I don't know,' she said slowly. 'I'll be very tact-ful.'

'My darling—you couldn't be if you tried. You're much too honest. The truth is sacrosanct to you.'

'Oh—there are ways around things. Often one has to tell a patient only half truths, as you know.'

'Yes . . .' he heaved a sigh. 'I know.'

Something in the face of the other drew them in-stinctively together as, with a groan, she was dragged into his arms and kisses rained down over her face and throat, so that she too was caught up in Paul's passion, revelling in his male dominance as her hands slipped behind his head and then there was just the discovery of an even greater dimension of their new loving; each holding on to a fine thread of control. She hadn't known she was even capable of so much depth of feeling—of longing and wanting. But it was he who presently released her and stood up, running his fingers through his hair while he breathed very deeply, before smiling down at her ruefully.

'I think, my sweet, that I'd better get us both some more coffee,' he said, leaning to kiss her bruised lips, but lightly this time. 'Then—I shall drive you straight home.'

She stretched lazily. 'If you say so, Dr Keslar. Oh, how did this happen to two people, never having seen each other until recently? I'm afraid it will go away again. Oh, Paul—it's so precious—we won't let it lose the quality or whatever . . . I couldn't bear to reduce what we feel for each other to an ordinary level.'

'Oh . . .' he said between laughter and a more serious tone 'was there ever a more intense, more wonderful girl than my Annabel . . .?' Then, resolutely, 'It's up to us, you know.' And pulling her to her feet, looked down into her face, 'We're going to take good care that nothing is spoiled between us. I love you—I've never said those words lightly, and never more seriously than now. 'I'm going to go on loving you, not less, but more as time goes on. Through all the ups and downs, this is a once and for all thing for me. We'll make it all happen, my darling, you and I; if you're very sure it's what you want too.'

'I'm very sure, Paul,' she said softly, tracing a line on his face. 'I love you and need you. I just want to be there, every day—helping you, making you happy. Nothing is ever going to change the way I feel about you. I'm glad you know now. I couldn't bear it when you didn't.'

'So, you can come and help me make the coffee . . .' he grinned, and his arm around her shoulders was enough just then.

They sat drinking it, hot and strong, and now she began to notice the room and decor, admiring the rather solid furniture, which, because there wasn't too much of it, didn't look cumbersome in the large room. The green velvet curtains were somewhat faded but it didn't seem to matter. The carpet too, of grey green, was also faded. He guessed her thoughts.

'You're wondering if it all belongs to me,' he said smiling across at her. 'No—I've taken it furnished. One or two things are mine, and the books, of course. I like it. It's a restful room to come back to after a day at the hospital. The kitchen, though small, is adequate, and the bathroom—which, by the way, is through that door—was a small dressing room, I should think. For the master of the house.'

'I wonder why the past has such a fascination. I love old houses,' Anna said wistfully. 'There is a lot of history in some of them around here. Did you know that?'

'Well—there is certainly a very mellowed atmosphere in some of the old villages. The church over there looks thirteenth century, though I haven't had time to see inside yet.'

'We must go, Paul,' she reminded him. 'Gran is alone in the house and it's getting late.'

'Of course. You also have to be up very early.'

'I love you . . .' It came from her depths.

He touched her mouth gently with his finger. 'You're like no other girl I know. Surprising and delicious . . .' he said tenderly. 'One moment a woman in love, deeply passionate. Your eyes tell me that. Oh, yes. I see them, not you. The next moment, you're like a child, wide-eyed and trusting.' He held her close. 'How did I come to find you, Anna?'

'I knew it first, Paul. I'm just so relieved that you loved me too . . .'

Gran had left the light on for them. He left Anna at the door and she watched dreamily as he walked quickly back to the gate in the light of a huge golden moon. The car engine died away. She locked up and climbed the spiral staircase, still bewitched by the sheer joy of being in love with Paul.

Her last waking thoughts were of him and his anxiety and commitments to his father. Somehow she had to make it possible to go with him to Wales. She wanted to share his background, see his home, but should she put Sister in the picture or not? Tomorrow, she would decide that.

Sister-in-Charge of Rowan looked up at her favourite staff nurse and gave her a searching look as she listened to her request.

'You would want Friday too, then? Does it have to be the 17th?'

'Yes. I'm afraid it does, Sister. I wouldn't ask unless it was so important.'

'No—you're very adaptable usually, Staff. But Friday . . .'

'Perhaps just the afternoon. You see, I want to go to Wales . . .'

'Ah. With Dr Keslar, or shouldn't I ask?'

'Oh, dear. Yes, actually. You see . . .'

'Don't tell me; what you do outside of this hospital is entirely your own business, as long as I have no idea what's going on in my ward. I don't want to know.'

Anna said very quietly, 'Dr Keslar is taking me to meet his father, Sister. It isn't what you're thinking at all. I—didn't want to involve you, but we have nothing to hide; it's just not time yet.'

Sister spoke just as quietly. 'I'm sorry. Dr Keslar

is fairly new here. It was for his sake as well as your own. I believe he is coming up to consultancy level soon—you don't need me to tell you what this hospital grapevine is like. Very well—you may have your weekend—and quite honestly, I don't know whether to congratulate you or not, Staff.'

'No. Not yet. Please can we keep it entirely confidential, Sister?'

'I can—if you can,' she said with a mischievous smile, not often seen. 'Now—can you do Mr Piper's dressings right away. He's very uncomfortable, and then look at Mr Janes's incision so that I can give an up-to-the-minute report to Mr Lonsdale when he makes his round later.'

'Yes, Sister.'

A moment later she was back to ask, 'Can you spare a minute? There is some inflammation and his temp is up to 100.2°.'

'Right.' Sister bustled beside her to the patient in question. Two dedicated nurses with very different private lives away from the hospital, because Sister had an elderly mother who watched the clock for her return each evening. Deep down, Sister wondered why life was so blatantly unfair. Her own emotions, frustrated in the inevitability of her own life and pressures, while Anna's weekend meant that she would be with her lover. And he, every woman's idea of a perfect man. She could imagine them driving along the road to Wales—all that lovely scenery. Oh, how she envied them. She drew a deep sigh and straightened her dress and cap. She could hear the voices already in the corridor which heralded the approach of Mr Lonsdale and his retinue. Well— she was ready. The reports and notes to hand. She went to meet them.

CHAPTER EIGHT

THE next week skimmed by so quickly that Anna began to feel as if she were in a vacuum of happenings. Her work at the hospital, then coming home to find that Gran, stimulated by the exciting plans for the future, had promptly decided to have her flat redecorated, which of necessity involved Anna as well, because Jane Forster never did anything by halves. Paul came over twice during the week, staying for supper. Tim had promised to come for two nights at the weekend and Anna had to concede to his male ego, that he had been right all along.

When she asked if he could possibly come to keep Gran company he had replied,

'And why am I in such demand?'

'I—I've been asked to go to Wales and you know I can't leave Gran alone. She says Mrs Shears would come but that's almost as bad. Heaven knows what they might get up to. Do say you can, Tim. It's terribly important to me.'

'Okay. Latish on Friday, though.'

'Thanks. We're leaving around three. She won't mind a few hours. Oh—Tim—she's decorating . . .'

'Oh, no. But you said we . . .'

'Yes, I did. You see, Dr Keslar is taking me to meet his father. He's rather ill.'

'Is he now? I don't mean father—sorry about that. So—was I right? And is he going to be my brother-in-law then?'

'Tim . . .' she said, sharply for her. 'We haven't

got that far yet. It's very private, love. *Please* keep it under your hat.'

'But—if Gran knows.'

'She doesn't—more than you. And I haven't mentioned it to the parents yet.'

'Well—it will cost you. I'll have to ditch the most attractive girl I've met here, that's all. Suppose I couldn't bring her too?'

'I don't see why not,' she began doubtfully.

His deep laugh, to which she hadn't yet become accustomed, came over the wire. Not long ago he was still a schoolboy, or so it seemed.

'I'm only kidding. It's okay. You go and have fun. But I expect to be the first to know if there are any developments . . .'

'Such as . . .?'

'As if you didn't know. See you. Bye.'

Friday morning sped by too. Mr Lonsdale and Paul were around early and quite a few extra tasks came up which couldn't be delegated, so she seemed to work with one eye on the clock the whole time.

Baths, and backs and heels to be rubbed; it often needed two nurses to turn patients and hold. Beds to be changed. Patients to be discussed, report sheets to be completed, medication given and entered. And lunch—with a go-slow in the kitchen making it even more difficult.

But at one-thirty, with the co-operation of Sister and the rest of the staff, she finally escaped and drove back to the Oast House with her spirits soaring, given full rein by the time she reached home.

Paul was coming direct from the Royal to pick her up. His case was already in the car. She had seen his jacket on a hanger in the back, and he would no doubt change at the hospital.

The day was hot, but with a slight breeze, so clothes for her were no problem. She was ready just before three and came down into the lounge looking cool and fresh, wearing a pale yellow cotton dress with white sandals and shoulder bag to match.

Her lovely peach-coloured skin—because of a slight tan now—glowed, needing no make-up except a trace of lipstick and eye shadow. Her hair hung soft and silky to her shoulders. It had been brushed until it shone. She simply wanted to look good, for Paul. Anna never had been conceited about her appearance. She was just grateful for her assets, ate healthily, and the exercise on the wards did the rest for her figure.

She put down her light case, giving Gran a critical look. 'I hope you aren't overdoing things. Do let Tim help you get straight. The men are almost finished, aren't they? You know, you really are naughty to have chosen just this particular time to have all this done.'

'But it's the best time of all, especially if there's to be a wedding in the house.'

'Oh, Gran—no-one has said there is going to be one. You mustn't say anything about Paul and me to anyone.'

'Of course not, dear. But do allow me a share in the pre-plans. You have no idea what pleasure it gives me. I am so happy to see two people so in love, and one of them my grand-daughter. I'll be waiting to hear all about it on Sunday.'

Anna hugged her. At that moment she saw Paul's car nosing in through the gate and her heart quickened its beat. 'He's here.'

'Hullo. You're ready. Good,' he said, aware of Gran standing by, enjoying every minute of it. 'How are you, Mrs Forster?'

'I'm very well, Paul. Have a good weekend.'

'Thanks. I'm sure we will.'

'It's a long journey. You will take care?'

He looked at Anna and she saw the patient amusement in his eyes as he answered back. 'Yes, we'll take care.' They both waved while they could still see her standing there in her navy and white linen dress, with Shane beside her.

'You'll be like her, when you reach her age,' Paul observed. 'Ageless . . .'

She smiled, throwing back her head in the sheer joy of escapism, quite content to sit beside him and feel the breeze in her hair as she thought of the two whole days which she would spend with him.

Tonight, they would both be in the same house. There would be all the time in the world to say the things they hadn't been able to before. He heard her long, contented sigh.

'You look so happy,' he told her as they approached the ring road. 'No hang ups today?'

'I never have hang ups,' she said indignantly.

'Oh. Sorry. I thought—I'm only teasing.'

'I know that. I look happy because I am. Actually, I'm still recovering from a hectic morning—can't quite believe it yet. So are you, I expect. Did you get any lunch?'

'Just a bite. We'll stop somewhere later, but Mrs Hughes will have a meal ready for us when we arrive, so we had better be hungry. Dad will be watching the clock too. Maybe I shouldn't have taken an opening quite so far away from him, but one makes a decision and that's it. He wouldn't want it any other way.'

'I'm so looking forward to meeting him and seeing

your home. Two hundred miles beside you . . .'

'It's marvellous to have you right there next to me.' He reached for her hand, his fingers firm and sure, his touch making her close her eyes to the joy which ran through her body. To love someone this much was sheer heaven. She hadn't known it could be like this. Oh Paul, I love you so. But this was not the time to tell him as he withdrew his hand to manipulate a bend. Besides, the motorway traffic was fairly heavy and he needed full concentration to keep up a good speed.

'Normally I would avoid them; I prefer the secondary roads,' he said after they joined the M4 going west, 'but when time is the essential, this is the answer. We'll branch off at Ross-on-Wye though. I spent my holidays with my grandparents there. He, too, was a practitioner.'

'So—it's definitely a family leaning—you weren't persuaded into it? It was your own choice, Paul?'

'I don't see how anyone can be motivated into taking up surgery against his will,' he said thought-fully. 'It's too long and too frustrating before one ever reaches finals, and then the houseman syndrome is only the beginning. You just have to be studying every spare minute, not missing out anywhere, and liking what you're doing with your tongue between your teeth. I've been fortunate in my seniors—they've been of infinite help in every way. Even the unpredictably tempered ones. I've had opportunities for teach-ins which have proved invaluable. I know I've been very lucky to have got this far so soon.' He gave her a quick smile. 'You're a wonderful listener, my sweet. Good for my ego.'

'Thank you. But I don't call it luck, Paul. Every nurse, and the doctors, too, all praise your work.

They say you are a splendid surgeon. I can believe that. I only wish I could be in theatre with you sometime, but I seem to have taken root on Rowan. Perhaps I just might get up to the gallery when off duty and you're operating.'

'I think I prefer you not to be around when I'm in theatre,' he said seriously.

'Even if you didn't know I was there?'

'I'd know. Actually, theatre sister on three and her staff are the most efficient I have ever worked with. A surgeon has to rely so much on his team, and fortunately most theatre sisters know that and enjoy their work tremendously.'

'I know. It's odd, isn't it? It's the routine and precision and, let's face it, anticipating a surgeon's need for a certain instrument, having everything to hand, and . . .' she smiled wryly, 'not dropping anything. That's why it was so strange that day in O.P. I had never dropped anything during my six months in theatre—ever.'

He remembered retrospectively and smiled.

'Why did you come to Calderbury, Paul? From a large teaching hospital to a smaller, less well-equipped one, like the Royal?'

'There were reasons which . . .'

She stopped him. 'I shouldn't have asked. There's some professional etiquette involved, isn't there?'

'Yes. I can't disclose the procedure, Anna. Except I have seniority here which I needed and, of course, getting all the experience I can take in major surgery is more than just a step in the right direction. I'm enjoying my work here.'

'In fact, you are qualified to become a consultant if and when something comes up, is that it, Paul?'

'You know—we're talking shop,' he reminded her gently.

'I'm sorry. Oh! Couldn't we stop there for some tea?'

'Tea for you—coffee for me, and some of those delicious scones. Okay?'

'Lovely. Let's have it in the garden.'

After their short stop, they again took the road across country, passing through Ross, Paul pointing out special places he remembered. A wistaria-covered grey house, where his folks had lived; a hill he used to climb; the river where he caught his first fish. She shared it all with him. This was another man, his frown of concentration had disappeared already and the boyishness that every man has tucked away somewhere was showing through.

'We're heading for home now, Anna,' he told her as the signposts listed the miles still to go.

'Won't you let me drive for a bit? Just to give you a rest, Paul?'

He shook his head. 'I'm more used to the route, and I do enjoy driving. Perhaps on the way back.' He glanced at the watch on his wrist. 'We should make it before eight.'

She settled back to enjoying the scenery slipping by. Neither of them talked, but it didn't matter. There was a lovely feeling of togetherness.

At ten minutes to eight, he said with a note of excitement, 'When we get around that mountain, you will be able to see the house.'

They were on a road running around and half-way up a hill, and far down were fields of corn in a valley. 'Is that really a mountain? I thought it just another hill. It's covered with grass. How on earth do they keep it so short?'

He laughed, shaking his head. 'Sheep, of course.

They graze up there all year round. And it's much higher than you think, my love.'

She leaned forward as the car rounded the bend. A small gravel road wound down into the valley. She saw a white-arched bridge spanning a wide stream, the water sparkling in the evening sun, and then the house, white against the lea of the hill, looking as if it had nestled there for ever. Sheep were dotted about all over the slopes, parts of which were shadowed where the sun no longer reached.

'Paul, what a heavenly spot . . .' she breathed, moving closer against his shoulder. 'I can't see another house anywhere.'

'The village lies a mile and a half in that direction and there are two cottages where the shepherds live. You can't see them yet. They're behind the trees.'

'How on earth do those sheep get all up there?'

He grinned. 'When I was small, I asked that question and was told by old Llewellen that sheep in Wales have two short legs in front. I'm afraid I believed it until I could work it out for myself. I love this view of the house. We'll have to go out of the way a bit to get round to the back. I expect they've seen us. Yes—I can see Bronwen waving. She's in Dad's room—there—with the french windows open. Wave back . . .'

She did so, leaning forward in her impatience to arrive now.

Both Browen and Mrs Hughes were waiting on the gravel drive when they drove in, greeting Paul with obvious pleasure, both forming their first impressions of the girl he had brought home with him, the first girl ever.

'So it must be serious . . .' they had told each other over the tea cups that afternoon.

'This is Anna.' He looked so proudly at her that her heart melted once again while Paul, getting their cases from the car, could see that they both approved, ushering her inside, chattering all the time. He stopped for a quick word with Bronwen before taking her in to meet his father.

'He's waiting for you and I think you will see for yourself,' she told him quietly. 'I've got him back into bed again.'

Taking Anna's hand in his, Paul went into his father's study-bedroom. Her heart contracted and emotion gripped her throat as she saw the affection between them and the poignancy of the situation. Because there would not be many more opportunities to be together. He was supported by several white hand-embroidered pillows; silver-haired with Paul's firm bone structure across his forehead.

'So this is Anna . . .'

She went forward now, almost shyly, for him to see her. 'How are you, Dr Keslar?'

He inclined his head. She was a nurse. No need for explanations even if he could have given them. 'I'm glad—you could come—with my son, Anna. I was curious to see you.' And to Paul, 'She's—a—lovely—girl—as you said . . .'

The excitement had exhausted him. His eyes closed against his will.

'Much pain, Dad?'

He nodded. 'Sometimes . . .'

'Get some rest now. We're going to eat. Mrs Hughes has a meal waiting, but after supper I'll be back.'

'Good.' It was an effort. Anna quietly went out into the hall leaving Paul to follow. There had been a small wood fire in the grate and one lamp glowed softly. It was a quiet room, she decided; a homely room with warm red-papered walls and lots of books and a red carpet. A room where Dr Keslar would be happier than anywhere else, among his leather arm-chairs and pictures which caught the fireglow on this summer evening, and Paul was right not to have him hospitalised.

She looked out through the open doorway of the hall. The sun had gone and a low, misty drizzle shrouded the hills. When Paul came to join her and led her into the dining-room, Bronwen followed them in.

'What do you think, Paul?' she asked softly.

'Much as you and Dr Williams, Bronwen. Will you tell Mrs Hughes we're ready. Unless, Anna, you'd like to freshen up first and see your room.'

'I'll only be a few minutes. I would, please.'

'Bronwen will show you.'

'This way, then.' She went with the quiet, capable nurse up the red patterned staircase and into her room which overlooked the valley.

'The bathroom is next door. If there is anything you need, don't hesitate to ask. You can find your way down, can't you?'

'Yes. Thank you, Bronwen. I may call you that?'

'Bless you, of course. So you're a nurse too! Staff, Paul says. Natural—that is.'

Anna nodded. 'So if I can help in any way, while we're here. Please ask me. Or if you want to go out over the weekend. I am sure Paul and I could cope. When do you have time off?'

'Not often. But it isn't for very much longer, is it? So it doesn't seem important somehow, does it?'

After they had eaten the beautifully cooked and served meal, she said that she would be in her

room if Paul needed her, getting her things unpacked.

'I know you'd like to be with your father. I expect
Bronwen gets him comfortable for the night soon and
he will want to have you to himself.'

She slipped her fingers inside his palm for a
moment. 'I'll be waiting, when you want me . . .'

'I—always want you,' he said, roughly for him,
crushing her hand in his.

'Good.' Her eyes were teasing until she saw his
darkening pupils and the muscles tense. Then, with
just a quick hug he went out and across the hall and
she heard his quiet tones as she went upstairs, still
wondering and dreaming a little.

Ten minutes later she was down. A light burned
in the lounge and an electric fire had been switched
on in the old-fashioned hearth. She stood at the
french windows watching the night descend among
the hills. The mist seemed to float like an ethereal
veil. This was Paul's home. She felt closer to him
here; sharing his background, the staples of his life.
Like a dream unfolding. She loved the way he had
looked today. Fawn slacks fitting his slim but well-
defined male form, a thin cream shirt moulding his
chest and back so that she saw the muscles ripple
and more than ever felt very aware that only he
could attract her physically so that she became conscious that she was waiting to be alone with him
again. Shyly, she had hidden this from him today.
She wasn't yet used to the clamour of her senses, the
shock waves along her nerves when she was near
him. Was this the transient period before two people
who needed each other so much made their love
come to fruition? Belonging. Yes—that was it. She
wanted desperately to belong to Paul. But he hadn't

said that yet. Only that he loved her and wanted her too.

I don't care, she thought desperately. Don't you see—I don't care about the future; about getting married. I only want us to be together. Anything you ask of me Paul . . .

But she knew she would never say this. There was still the line beyond which she couldn't go. She couldn't bear to see that withdrawn expression on his face again. She must wait for him to sort out his own plans first. But loving this way was certainly a painful business and, in her impulsive way, she wanted to rush right in. Instead, Paul was treading carefully. She remembered the night in his flat, smiling tenderly. She knew what it would be like, when the right time came.

She opened the doors and went out into the cool, damp night, still thinking retrospectively, loving the quiet hills all around. Her face cooled now. She could see Mrs Hughes in her small sitting-room off the kitchen, watching the television screen, but in Dr Keslar's room the curtains were now drawn. She imagined Paul there with his father and sadness mixed with pleasure at being together again. Then, realising that she was cold and damp, the cardigan around her shoulders not enough to stop it penetrating her bare arms, she turned back.

Paul was just closing the french window. 'Heavens—what are you doing out there? It's too damp. And you left the window open. Mrs Hughes put the fire on too.'

'Don't be cross. It was silly of me. But there was a kind of magnetism out there. I just walked into it.'

He drew her close. 'I just didn't know you were out there, that's all. Come on over to the fire. I'll get us a drink. Whisky be all right?'

'Yes. I just think it might. Thank you.'

While he was getting it, she looked around the comfortable room with no particular colour scheme or pattern, but which had lived through a marriage. It bore the imprint of two people at the end of the day, in well-worn armchairs; two photographs of Paul; one when he graduated and the other a smiling boy around twelve in his school uniform.

Anna picked it up, studying it closely, another glimpse into Paul's background, the part she didn't know. He came to stand beside her. 'I'd forgotten that.'

She looked up and the light caught her hair, giving it a spun texture. Her eyes caught and held by his, almost disbelieving what he saw as he turned her round to him, holding her face in both hands, as he bent to kiss her quickly parted lips. Then, drawing her close, his head above hers, she heard him say huskily, 'Oh—my Anna—you are so lovely—what am I going to do about us?'

'What . . .' she murmured, 'do you suggest, Dr Keslar?'

Again he bent to kiss her, his mouth tracing hers teasingly, until she could bear it no longer and, imprisoning him with her lips, intuitively, because she had never done anything remotely like it before, she felt him tremble against her.

He was surprised, but motivated too now, and his kiss reached into her very depths so that neither of them heard the door open and Mrs Hughes' shoes on the polished floor boards.

It hadn't occurred to her to knock first. It was embarrassing for her and certainly for Paul when he noticed her. His, 'What is it, Mrs Hughes?' made Anna break away too.

'I—just wanted to know if you would like anything else, before I go to my bed.'

They had recovered quickly. 'No, thank you, Mrs Hughes.'

'Breakfast at eight, as usual then?'

'That will be fine.'

'Do you want tea in bed?'

'Not for me. But I expect Anna might.'

'That would be a luxury. But I expect I'll be down for it, Mrs Hughes.' She was smiling and more composed now

'I'll say goodnight, then. You will remember to switch off the fire, won't you?'

'Of course. Goodnight.'

She closed the door very discreetly.

'Oh, dear . . .' Paul chuckled. 'I feel as if I've been caught kissing on the back porch after school.'

'Me too. She did look rather shocked, Paul.'

'I expect she quite enjoyed it.'

She had carried her drink to the window. He came to stand beside her.

'You really are fascinated by all that out there, aren't you?'

'Mmm. I get the feeling that those hills know a thing or two—they have a way of cutting one down to size.'

'And I should know,' he said, with his arm around her shoulders tightly. 'I was brought up with them. Do you want to go to bed?'

She caught her breath. 'What a suggestion, Dr Keslar.'

'Everyone else has.'

'And I expect you're tired. It was a long drive and after a hard morning.'

'So—shall we?'

She nodded, watching from the doorway as he turned off the switches.

Then they went upstairs together and, outside her door, he kissed her good and hard, but very finally as he whispered, 'Goodnight—it's unusual for me to turn in while my eyes are still open; but tonight, yes—with you in the next room.'

'Oh, Paul . . .' They were both aware of the quiet in the old house. She slipped into his arms and raised her mouth to his.

'God, I want you so much, Anna,' he whispered, then, silenced by her finger on his lips as she drew away, resolutely.

'I want you too,' she said softly, 'but not this way.' Then she was inside her room and he on the outside. A moment later his door closed too.

It was strange lying there in a different bed from her own, very conscious of Paul's nearness in the next room. Mutual love and respect for each other, and the fact that this was his father's house, and their own more intellectual outlook, kept them apart that night. But if it had been anywhere else, a hotel room perhaps, she knew that he would have come to her and she would have reached out for him lovingly, passionately.

Her thoughts broke off forcibly. She dared not pursue them further, imagining Paul's caresses, his body close to hers, without which she knew now she would always be incomplete.

She threw back the covers next morning to find a perfect summer morning spreading over the green vista of grass and fir trees which grew thickly up the slopes of Paul's other mountain around which they had driven yesterday.

She pulled on her white housecoat and went down to the kitchen, imagining herself to be up first, but Mrs Hughes was already there, teapot in hand, about to pour hers, intending to bring it upstairs.

'Paul is already up and out,' she announced. 'Gone up the hill, I shouldn't wonder. He likes to do that before breakfast. Did you sleep well?'

'Marvellously. Thank you, Mrs Hughes. No—no biscuits. I think I'll get dressed and go to find him. Which way is the hill?'

'Oh—you can't miss it, deed to goodness. Down the path, over the bridge and just start going up.'

'Ah—now I know I'm in Wales,' Anna said smilingly. 'You have a gorgeous accent.' Mrs Hughes was immediately captivated by that smile, as every patient on the receiving end had been too.

Quickly washing and dressing in blue slacks and a pale blue shirt, with her hair piled on top, she ran downstairs calling 'Good morning,' to Bronwen as she was about to enter Dr Keslar's room.

The door was already open, letting in a stream of early morning sun. She ran down and across the bridge, stopping to watch for a minute the clear water coming down from the hills and gurgling over the stones. She couldn't see Paul as she commenced climbing, her legs aching after a little time, but when she stopped to look back, the scenery was breathtaking and she knew why he wanted to go up even higher. Now she could see two cottages above the trees, set in the lea of the hillside and, further over, a hill farm and beyond the chimney pots and roofs of the village.

But where was Paul? Except for the sheep, there was no movement. It was quiet and lonely up there. But it didn't bother her. This was Paul's home. In the man she adored she saw the boy, exploring his old haunts. A far cry from his years in the London hospital and, now, Calderbury Royal. He had chosen his training ground well, and even now he was paving the way for his consultancy of the future. Here was his safety valve; where the pressures were gone. Pressures every doctor lives with daily, whether part of a hospital faculty, or a practitioner.

'Good morning.' His voice broke into her thoughts, echoing down the hillside. She looked up, shading her eyes, and saw him coming down to her. His hair was windblown and with a healthy glow in his cheeks, stumbling down the hill boyishly, he looked amazingly different from the white-coated groomed figure who walked the hospital corridors, usually wearing a thoughtful expression, quiet and decisive; and hiding his other self from everyone, but her. This man had no hesitation in giving her a bear hug and crushing her mouth with his in no uncertain way.

'You taste of morning dew—and you look so good. I can see you've enjoyed your climb.'

'It was great. Do you like my hill, darling? And how did you sleep?'

'Very well . . .'

'Good. I met Llewellen—he was up there training a new collie. You can see where he lives. It's good to do this sometimes. Come home. Gee—I'm hungry!'

'Me too. Race you to the bottom.'

They arrived for breakfast looking perfectly happy and the two women exchanged glances after Paul had gone to see his father and Anna had gone up to her room.

'I wish they could be married while he's still with us,' Bronwen said wistfully. 'I don't hear they're even engaged, or anything yet.'

'They're really in love though; you can see it, can't you? We may hear something before they go back to Kent or wherever it is.'

During the afternoon, while Bronwen went to the village, Anna and Paul stayed with Dr Keslar.

Perhaps, because she was a trained nurse, he accepted her ministrations without protest. He was very ill and had no illusions about the stage reached already in this crippling and, for him, incurable disease. Everything had been tried that could be; there had been relapses and remissions; now he was just too tired to fight the pain any more.

'Paul—has been telling me about your home. An oast house. You tell me, Anna—I—can think about it—after you've gone.'

'Tell Dad about your grandmother, Anna. He would just love her, wouldn't he?'

'I'm afraid she would simply take over—but she's a wonderful person, Dr Keslar. Have you ever been to Kent?'

They saw that he had fallen asleep.

Next morning, Anna again stood in for Bronwen who had taken a rare opportunity to go to Chapel, Paul driving her there, to her great pleasure.

When Anna came in with the coffee tray, Paul was back, sitting in the window, one leg crossed over the other, reading bits of the Sunday paper to his father.

Suddenly he said, between sentences, 'I—hope you will keep this house going, Paul—I want to imagine my grandchildren here some day. It makes sense—that way.'

Paul got up and went to the bed and sat down. He was very moved, as Anna saw.

'Dad. This house will be here, because of you. I'll never sell it, if that's what you're thinking. It means as much to me, you know.'

'And Anna? Does she like it?'

'I love it,' she said softly.

'That's settled, then. Everything else—has been taken—care of.' He grimaced.

'Dad—you're talking too much. Would you like an injection?'

'Time for that—when you've gone. These wretched spasms!'

The drive back to Kent took longer than on the way down and already Paul was trying to work out when he could do it again.

Neither of them mentioned that she had been included in the future of the house. It was all too sad.

'Has it depressed you, Anna?' Paul glanced at her unusually sober expression. 'I hope you don't regret coming.'

'I'm glad, Paul. I just wish I could have known him before . . .'

'He thinks you're someone very special—and so do I.'

'Oh . . .' impulsively she reached to touch him.

'I'd like to ask you to marry me.'

She couldn't speak.

'You knew that, didn't you?'

She shook her head. Tears were not far away. She felt emotionally overcharged.

He drew the car alongside a grass verge just off the road and turned to face her.

'You know that I love you—and want you, more than anyone else; that you've become a part of my life now. I'm not exactly struggling; but I have so little to offer you, darling. In wordly goods, that is. My finances are such that I couldn't even buy you a home. I think the moment of truth has come, and I have to say this to you.'

'Thank you.' She touched his face. 'Please ask me to marry you, just the same. I can't bear it, if you don't.' Her whisper ended in his kiss.

After a time, she said reasonably, 'We couldn't rush into it anyway—for a time, Paul. Couldn't we just enjoy this kind of prelude? I am quite sure that it will all happen for us. Just love me darling—and let me love you, until then.'

CHAPTER NINE

Tim had already left when their car drew up in front of the Oast House. It was after nine o'clock and both Paul and Anna were glad to stretch their stiffened muscles when they got out. But none of that mattered as he, with one arm slung round her shoulders and the other carrying her case, walked with her to where Gran waited in the kitchen porch.

'Were you getting worried?' Anna asked, kissing her. 'We are a bit later because the traffic was appalling . . .'

'No. Just getting a little anxious, perhaps. Do come in, Paul. What do you feel like? Supper? A drink first?'

'You're wonderful,' he told her, but looked at Anna for support.

She saw that a cold meal was ready on the table. 'Both, I think,' unable to keep the exhilaration from her voice. Gran heard the tremble of emotion and guessed what was coming.

'Let's have some sherry first or whatever because, you see, we have something to tell you.'

'Are you . . .?'

'We're going to be married, yes, sometime in the near future, but no dates yet. There's no hurry anyway. So now you're happy, aren't you? You old romantic . . .'

'Oh, my dears, yes.' She had to kiss them both, which Paul seemed to enjoy; her eyes were very bright.

They told her, while they ate supper, their reasons, up to a point, why they chose to wait for a while.

'I'm so sorry about your father's illness, Paul. I realise the extra strain this puts on you. Are you going to tell your parents? They must be in on this too,' she asked Anna.

'We'll phone them tonight.' She turned to Paul. 'I do wish they could meet you. I suppose there's no way that you could come with me. No—of course not—any holiday will be spent with your father, naturally. Perhaps at Christmas when they come home again.'

'It's a very tempting thought, darling. You're off at the end of the month, aren't you? I wonder—I know that Mr Lonsdale is going abroad at the end of September and Peter, who also works with Mr Lonsdale's registrars, is off next week. Leave it with me, will you? Even for a few days it would be worth it.'

'But—your father, Paul. Iceland is out of bounds, as it were . . .'

'I think he will be fairly stable for the next two months, Anna. I had a word with Dr Williams while at home. He doesn't think we can expect more than that, neither do I.'

'Oh, Paul—so soon?'

'He would want me to go with you, but that isn't the point, is it? Less than three weeks now. Why not wait until tomorrow to ring your parents? I may have been able to finalise something by then.'

'That's a good idea. I know they would be over the moon if I got off the plane with you. Besides, I wouldn't have to leave you behind.'

'All right,' he said slowly, taking out his diary. 'Just give me your flight dates and times—and your flight number. There just might be a spare seat on that one. Icelandair, isn't it?'

She nodded, her eyes like stars.

'I don't expect that everyone wants to go to Iceland anyway,' Gran broke in practically.

'Well,' Paul put his head on one side consideringly, 'I think it is becoming more popular as a holiday country more recently. It depends what you want, of course. I know that I would very much like the chance to see it. Your parents are at Reykjavik, I think you said, Anna.'

'Mmm.'

'Do we need a visa?'

'No.' He had to smile at her tenderly then, which Gran enjoyed too, because Anna sat at the table, chin in hand, watching him adoringly. Suddenly, her happiness was too much; she felt intoxicated with all that had happened. But now, he pulled her to her feet saying that he must go.

'If you'll both excuse me—there are one or two things I have to check on before I turn in. Monday morning will be with us too soon.'

He said goodnight to Gran, leaving her in a happy state of anticipation as she began to clear the table after Anna had gone out to his car with him. Life was made up of dreams and, sometimes, they came true. She had enjoyed a happy weekend with her grandson, and now this. But of course, she hadn't been at all surprised. They were just made for each other.

Anna climbed the staircase when the kitchen was finished and everything ready for the morning, feeling exhausted, both physically and mentally. Bed seemed the sensible next move. Monday on Rowan

was always a busy day and she needed to be alert
and re-charged for it.

Besides, she wanted to be alone. To re-think over
the time which she had spent with Paul. To remember. 'I want to marry you, Anna,' he had been
so very serious about that. To re-capture his kisses,
his touch—oh, the ecstasy of his hands caressing her,
the flare of passionate longing each time they were
close. 'Oh, Paul—I do love you so much,' she whispered, as she brushed her hair in front of her mirror.
I look different, she thought. Everything looks different. Paul's wife, oh, she knew just what it would
be like to be married to him; she would never let
him down. He would be proud of her—she would
help him in every way she could, and love him
always. She couldn't not love him; only, how could
she wait for that time?

It was more than usually hectic on the ward next
day. Sister had had a bad weekend and didn't en-
quire after Anna's at all, which seemed significant.
Even the patients were extra gloomy, facing another
week of hospitalisation. One patient in the small
room had to be specialled and while Anna couldn't
be released for this, she had to keep an eye on the
second-year nurse who had been designated for the
task. In the middle of the morning, Mr Lonsdale
sent one of his outpatients up to the ward to be
admitted, which meant that someone had to take
particulars, get him into bed, weighed, urine checked
and Dr Lancing called to re-examine, before he was
put on the ward list officially. And Sister decided that
the linen cupboard, a small room actually, must have
every shelf checked and tidied by mid-afternoon.

Apart from which, Anna registered as she went

silently about other jobs to be got through, there were thirty-five patients to receive attention in one way or another and be reported upon, leaving out extras.

No time to think of anything remotely personal, but, because she was brim-full of happiness inwardly, her smile was soon back and her feet light as she pushed on. The third-year nurse from Gynaecology proved an asset, relieving Anna of the need to supervise once she saw the efficient way she went about her work.

Just before five, Paul and Dr Lancing came into the ward. He made straight for her desk, when he saw that Sister was absent.

'Hullo. We'd just like to have a look at Mr Stephens. You have the test results?'

'Yes, Dr Keslar.'

'I'll put them with his notes.' Erika Lancing took them and, telling Anna that they could manage, went over to the bed, leaving Paul and Anna at the table.

He said quickly, 'I'd like to come over tonight, if I may. I think I have good news on both points.'

'To supper?'

He shook his head. 'No. I have a meeting at seven. Later—on my way home.'

'See you then. Oh—could you initial this for me?' He scribbled his name quickly then said 'Goodbye,' in a low voice, thrilling her with its intimate tone.

How different from the diplomacy needed at the Royal was the scene that evening when she ran to meet him across the lawns of the Oast House, Shane barking at her side.

'What a welcome . . .' he said laughingly, as he got out of his car and reached for her hand.

'You look tired,' her eyes saw it at once.

'Well—yes; I suppose so. But I have good news. Cook's have got me on to your flight. So we fly out together on the Saturday morning.'

'Oh, that's marvellous, Paul. I really must phone Iceland tonight. What about right now? Come and say hullo to them, won't you?'

Her voice trembled as she told her parents about Paul and the eyes she raised to his were emotionally bright. Eve and Ralph were delighted and wanted to talk to him. In contrast, his voice was more controlled as he asked them to book him into a hotel near their home for that week.

'But you must stay with us, of course,' Eve told him. They could hear the excitement in her voice too.

'No question about it,' Ralph put in. 'We're both looking forward to meeting you. We'll be there when your plane gets in.'

She slipped into Paul's arms when the phone had been put down, content to stay close while their thoughts ran on ahead separately. Then Anna decided to make some coffee, admitting that she felt a little overwhelmed by it all. 'Do you?'

'No. I don't think so. Happy—yes.'

'Paul . . .' she stood with the coffee pot in her hand, 'we don't have to make any announcements, do we? I'd like to keep it to ourselves for a while.'

'It would be less traumatic,' he agreed, coming up behind her, his hands circling her waist, 'but I suppose we're engaged now, aren't we? I should buy you a ring.'

'No,' she said, shaking her head. 'Not yet, anyway. I'd much rather you used that money for your air fare.'

'Oh—my practical Anna. I shall do something about your ring—at the right time. Did I tell you that I have to go down to Cardiff for a seminar next weekend? I'll probably go on and see my father for a few hours afterwards. As I have to lecture, I shan't be free until Sunday. I'll call you from home.'

'I'll miss you, but you'll enjoy the seminar. One never seems to stop talking at those gatherings.'

'I know. One tries to cram so much into too short a time.'

'You have to work on it beforehand, I expect.'

He nodded. ' 'Fraid so. I'm almost there—just another hour or so.'

She felt bereft after he had left on Friday. But she was already preparing for the holiday and because Paul was coming too, clothes seemed to have greater significance. She knew he noticed what she wore and she wanted him to feel proud of her. Leaving the house empty too would mean extra chores beforehand.

When Paul phoned on Sunday, she felt a physical urgency for him to return. He said very little about his father for obvious reasons, but she sensed that he was worried.

When she saw him he was accompanying Mr Lonsdale on his rounds, with the rest of his medical team in the party. There was no way they could talk. But she stood beside the other nurses, listening, admiring, adoring him; as he moved from one bed to the next.

He drove out to the Oast House that evening, just as the sun was going down in a red ball of fire over the hill.

'I'm so glad you came.'

'I thought we might finalise plans for the weekend—and for this, of course,' he murmured, as he kissed her, lingering over her lips with his, so that she was drowning in the sensations he aroused deep within her body.

'Oh—Paul—when I least expect it . . .' she couldn't look at him.

He grinned wickedly. 'Ah—you see—you don't know me very well yet, do you, Staff Nurse? But, you will . . .'

Friday came at last. She drove home humming along with the tune in her mind. Paul too would be packing tonight. They were leaving early next morning for Heathrow.

Already Shane was at the kennels; she had taken him on her way to the hospital, having to steel herself not to let the look of reproach he gave her as he was led away deter her. But now she missed him coming to meet her as she put her car in the garage for the next two weeks. So much would have happened in that time. She couldn't envisage the happiness she and Paul would share; and her parents' impressions of him. Oh—she was so proud to be taking him to meet them for the first time.

Everything went according to plan next day. They reached the airport in good time and when the blue and white jet left the runway and began to climb, Anna felt exhilarated at once.

In minutes, or so it seemed, they were over the Atlantic.

'You look like a small girl going on a birthday treat,' Paul told her indulgently.

'Oh—no. Is it that obvious? You see, I've never flown before.'

'Really? I wouldn't have known.'

'You're teasing.'

'Oh—Anna—you're so refreshing. This is a short flight—two hours, I think; but long flights can be painfully boring.'

She slipped off the jacket of her green suit when the hostess arrived to serve coffee or drinks, enjoying the cool feel of her soft cream shirt against her skin. There was a marvellous sense of intimacy in being next to Paul like this; except for Wales, she couldn't feel free; conceding that the hospital would always come first, because of his profession necessarily so, separating them because of his status; but not today. Nothing could.

'After this, we shall have many shared experiences, I hope, Anna. This is the beginning.'

'I know. That is what is so exciting. Not knowing. I wouldn't want to. I think an element of surprise keeps one on tip-toe. I'm happy when we're together.'

'You know,' he spoke quietly, 'if I didn't know that you were such a perfect nurse, with all the adherent discipline and responsibilities, demands, and, if I hadn't seen you coping with some very nasty emergencies, I would think you quite the most naive girl I had ever known. I can only conclude that you have a simple code of happiness which is enviable. You're quite uncomplicated and . . .' he whispered against her hair, 'I adore you.'

'You don't have to whisper with all this noise,' she said. Conversation buzzed like insects throughout the cabin. But he saw her eyes glisten with the suspicion of a tear as she turned to look down through the billowing clouds, to a tiny patch of blue sea, far below.

After two hours the 'Fasten seat belts' sign went up and a general stirring among the passengers as they complied.

The plane dropped and began its descent through the clouds, hovering over the island before it finally went in to land.

But they had seen Iceland from the air. A vast expanse of barren land, mountains and rocks, rivers and peaks. Anna had drawn in her breath at its unexpected beauty.

'The colours, Paul, I didn't expect it to look so beautiful. Like a jewel—in a blue setting. That must be Reykjavik.' The houses, as she peered from the small window, seemed very close together, but clean and separate; their roofs either red or pink or blue or green. There was the glint of a lake in the centre and some trees, but not many. Mountains stood sentinel, like slumbering guardians on the sea line.

'Not a bit as I expected,' she said again. 'It's lovely—a bit frightening though—so much naked land. Not densely populated, is it?'

He was looking over her shoulder. 'I read somewhere that only a sixth of the island is habited. Of course, it's very mountainous. A lot of water—lakes and rivers. But plenty of room to breathe, wouldn't you say, my sweet?'

'We're landing!' Her excitement became intense now. 'It will be good to see them. I expect they're just behind that barrier somewhere. Oh, I am glad you came too.'

Outside, the air was pleasantly warm and very clean and pure; exhilaratingly so.

As they went through the corridors of the airport terminal, they saw glass cases displaying Icelandic crafts. Furs, woollens in bright colours, wood and silver carvings.

Icelandic she knew was a difficult language to

learn, so Anna was delighted to realise that practically everyone spoke English because it was taught in the schools.

And then there were her parents, waving frantically as they waited behind the barrier when they turned the corner. Paul walked purposefully beside her while a porter wheeled their cases. Her eyes shone with happiness.

'Isn't he good-looking?' Eve murmured to her husband. 'They look good together, don't they?'

Ralph wasn't committing himself, finding that he had rather mixed feelings, realising, for the first time, that his small daughter had gone for good and this silk-shirted girl with fashionable high-heeled sandals coming towards him, was a slim and lovely woman. She had changed, even in the last few months. And that man by her side was the only one in her life now.

But then they were meeting; all talking at once; and Ralph was leading the way to his parked car. With Paul in front with him and Anna at the back with her mother, the car joined the traffic on the way out of town. She and her mother exchanged happy glances as the two men in front chatted, as men do, both feeling their way with the other. Her father, older, his hair silver streaked now, and Paul's darker, well-groomed—masculine.

'You're getting your first impressions of Reykjavik now,' Ralph was saying.

'My first, is of the absolute cleanliness everywhere.'

'It's a smokeless city, of course,' Ralph told him, turning on to a highway. 'This is Miklabraut, we're heading out of town now. There will be time to show you the town during the week. We hope you'll see as much as you can while you're here, Paul. You don't mind—I can't be calling you Dr Keslar all the time.'

'Of course not.' He glanced round at Anna. 'Besides, I hope I'm to be family soon.'

'We're very happy about it,' Ralph said. 'Just listen to those two in the back there. My wife is longing to celebrate. I think she's asked some friends in to meet you. We're almost there now. I think you'll appreciate the way the Icelandic people have really achieved something in their life style when you see where we live.'

They turned into a small drive. The house was square, with white paint and a red roof. Ralph got out and opened the solid door which led straight into a large room, with a light polished floor and bright rugs. It was a room full of clear colours with square wood chairs and cushions, one wall was filled with books.

'They were here,' Eve told them, 'every Icelander is a great reader. Probably, they are the most literate society in the world. And I have to admit, I do like their Scandinavian-design way of living. Do come and see my kitchen, Anna. Isn't it super? I love working here.'

It quite took Anna by surprise. 'Heavens—you have absolutely everything. It would cost a fortune back home. Like something out of *Homes and Gardens*.'

'I know. Come up and see your rooms. Paul, you too.' The two men were looking at the many wall pictures, but now he picked up their cases and followed them upstairs. Wooden too, with a solid rail. The bedrooms were plainly furnished, but adequate, but the bathroom was quite luxurious.

It seemed strange to see Paul unpacking his things

and hanging them in the wall cupboard. She went in. 'We're here,' she said softly, then, 'hold me—just for a second.'

They came down to find that Eve had a simple meal of wholemeal bread, smoked fish, cheeses, with golden butter, fruit and salad.

'That is Schnapps, Paul—actually, it's Brennevin. Like to try some—it's a bit lethal.'

'Yes. I will, thanks.'

He had poured wine for Eve and Anna and now they raised their glasses. '*Skol!* Which means, good health. We're none of us much use without that—but, to you both, much happiness.'

Again they raised their glasses and then Paul, thanking them, with his eyes on Anna, said quite out of context for him, 'I hope she will always look as happy as she does now.'

On Sunday, they drove out to Gullfoss, which has been called the most beautiful waterfall in the world. It certainly dwarfed them as they stood on the rock face watching it cascade down from a great height over three levels, catching the sun's rays, giving it rainbow colours as it roared into the gorges far below.

There were guests to supper that evening. When they arrived, Ralph introduced one couple as Dr Jön Erikson and his wife, Helga. 'Jön is a surgeon at the City Hospital, Paul. I know you will have some interest in each other's profession; and this is Magnus and Krista Sveinsson, who are our very good friends. Magnus and I are working together.'

Because they were all so compatible the evening passed too quickly. Paul had been invited to visit Jön at the hospital and Magnus wanted them to come for a meal sometime. They were surprised and disappointed when he said that he must return home at the end of a week.

On Monday they swam in warm pools, naturally heated from the hot springs, toured the town, stood on the harbour and looked across at the Mount Esja, slumbering guardian-like over the city. Drove by an old Nordic house reflected in the shining lake, blue in the reflection of clear skies. The trees on the out-skirts of the town—and the peace—almost tranquil, in the warm, soft air. The museums and buildings—and everyone seeming to have work of some kind.

'What an industrious lot they are,' Paul observed.

And late that night, they looked out over a gold and grey sea; the little boats at anchor. Anna and Paul, hand in hand, feeling the release from work tensions sliding away at last. They had dined at a hotel—eaten delectable food; danced a little, and now were on their way home. Anna's dress ruffled in the soft breeze, touched his dark suit. They stood so close together that Eve felt a lump in her throat. 'They're perfect together,' she said softly to her hus-band.

'So are we.'

'You old romantic. Let's go home. It's late.'

'Just after midnight, that's all.'

'And like a summer morning at home,' Anna said. 'It really is true—about the Land of the Midnight Sun.'

'Of course,' her father said, smiling. 'We're in the Gulf Stream here, you know. It's never really cold and sometimes, like this evening, really warm. Tomorrow, I think we'll go to Thingvella—unless you have other plans. It's National Land, but ex-tremely beautiful; fields, lakes and rivers and perhaps you'd like to see some hot springs.'

The whole of the next day was taken up with travelling from one place to another—they watched hot mud bubbling beneath the surface, saw snow-capped mountains; sailed around the coast for two hours, returning through Reykjavik to the bright little house in the evening, tired, but healthier than they had felt for months.

Ralph had planned to take them to the shores of Hvalfjördur and then drive on to Akranes on Wednesday.

'Up to the more rugged areas. There is so much contrast. You can't come to Iceland and not see the ice fields and glaciers around Eriksjókull. There are some interesting craters too.'

'Ralph,' Eve said gently, 'Perhaps they would prefer to go somewhere else? Shopping?'

'No.' Both Anna and Paul protested. 'We'd like to see as much as we can before Paul has to leave. Mum and I can go to the shops next week,' she finished.

'Then I suggest we take an overnight bag and stay somewhere. There are several possible stopovers. I really think that Paul would enjoy the phenomena—apart from the scenery.'

'That will only leave Friday,' he said ruefully. 'Yes—I think we must do this route. It's very good of you to want to drive that far.'

It was a heavenly morning when they set off from Reykjavik, stopping for a break at the mouth of a fjord and then on to Bórganes for lunch.

Afterwards, they drove along by rushing, ice-blue waters, then inland and up towards heather-covered downs, backed by a snow-capped mountain. Ralph parked the car.

'Up there is a lava field,' he explained. 'We'll go round it, and I'll take you up to the crater.'

They set off on foot, having been warned to wear good strong shoes, the two men in front, Anna and her mother following.

'I'm afraid I don't really enjoy this kind of scenery,' Eve confessed, as her hair blew over her face in the strong breeze sweeping through the fjord. 'Much too rugged and stark. Too naked for me but, of course, your father is in his element. Do you think Paul is enjoying it?'

'Oh—I'm sure he is. But I do see what you mean. A bit frightening, isn't it?'

They went on climbing up the side of the roughened crater. Anna preferred the breathtaking and dangerous magnitude of Gullfoss, but after she had slipped a few times and saw the depth of the rocks, she realised that it was deceptively less so.

The men had reached the rim of the crater, their voices drifting back to them. Suddenly Anna said, 'I don't think I want to go all up there, do you? It rather gives me the creeps. It's all so grey and stark.'

'I know. In contrast to all that colour down there. We'll wait here.'

She called up to Ralph, so she heard, rather than saw, Anna's slithering shoes as she tried to regain her balance. One moment she had been upright, the next she had slipped on the slate-like rock face—and now, to her horror, she was out of control, crashing over on to the ledge beneath. She heard her mother's scream through the sound of the wind in her ears;

Paul's, 'My God—Anna!'

Her father's shout, 'Hold on!'

Her hands were bleeding, her torn nails clutching at anything, frantically, which jutted; but her merciless slithering continued timelessly. Her head hit the side of a crevice in the rock and she dropped into the blackness of the ravine.

CHAPTER TEN

ANNA never knew what happened next, or that Paul was the first to reach the long wide crack in the rock. He lay full length, calling her name, until Ralph arrived, white-faced, thrusting his torch into the blackness. Until then, there was no way of knowing how far she had fallen—it could be bottom-less—nor if she was still alive even. Shock gripped him in spite of his training for just such an accident.

'I can see her. She's on a ledge. She can't fall any more, thank God—there's just a crack—not wide enough to let her through. She's unconscious, Paul. Hold on to my wife—she might pass out. I'm going for help. Now, we passed a farmhouse; they'll have a phone. The rescue team should be here in half an hour. Nothing to do but pray now. I'll leave the torch. For God's sake, hang on to something, both of you.'

He wasted no more words. Soon his yellow car was threading its way down the winding road far below. Eve sat very still, shocked, trembling inwardly. Paul, still holding her hand, lay down full length, running the torch around the gulley with his other hand. His heart plumetted when he saw the splintered rock. There was blood on Anna's white face. No sound. Again, he called her name. 'Oh, my darling.' Eve heard the anguish in his voice and started to cry, struggling against his hold.

'We can't do anything at all, until the rescue team get here. Please keep very still.'

'But . . .'

'She isn't feeling any pain,' he said gently.

It seemed an age, but was barely half an hour, before they both saw the land-rover speeding up the narrow road, followed by Ralph's yellow car.

'Thank God,' Paul said quietly. Anna would have recognised his 'emergency' voice.

'They're here.' The men had started up over the rocks carrying ropes and a stretcher.

'Stay where you are, won't you?' He let go of her hand.

'But I want to help. I must do something.'

'None of us can do anything, until she is brought up.'

'Oh—please let her be alive,' Eve sobbed, distraught now.

He gripped her shaking hands. Ralph came on behind the others, white and shocked too. He had brought brandy from the car. Paul made them both have some while the men worked with ropes. One of the team had already gone down. It seemed an eternity before Anna was brought up and gently put on the stretcher. Paul knelt beside her, lifting her eyelids, feeling for her pulse.

'She's alive,' he said briefly, too shaken for more words as his hands probed her body for the fractures he knew must be there.

One of the men wiped the blood and black, wet slime from her face, the first-aid box open. There was a deep gash from thigh to knee on one leg. Paul applied a tourniquet while the medically-trained team splinted the other leg.

'This arm too . . .' Paul said quietly. 'I'll bandage her head. How far to the hospital?'

'Akranes.'

'Can't wait for an ambulance, I'm afraid.'

'The rover is fitted for the stretcher, Doctor.'

'Good. I'll stay with her.'

'We'll follow,' Ralph said, gripping his wife's arm firmly, as they began the descent. He wanted to ask Paul's opinion but there was no time even to ask the question fearfully in both their minds.

Paul suspected a skull fracture, though he had no way of knowing definitely. He could only hope that there were no internal injuries. She seemed to have fallen on her side. Her lacerated body filled him with cold horror, even though he was trained for this; but because it was Anna.

His eyes never left her face as he sat beside her all the way to hospital.

How could this have happened—his lovely Anna? Why? He couldn't bear to see her blood-stained face, gaping cuts, which was all that was visible under the blue blanket.

While they waited, he put his head in his hands and prayed. At last a doctor came to tell them her suspected injuries, speaking mainly to Paul when he realised that he was a surgeon.

Twenty-four hours later, Anna opened her eyes, trying painfully to recognise the nurse sitting beside her bed in a strange hospital room. The blur cleared. Her lips were cracked and swollen. It was difficult to talk. Her voice sounded slurred, even to her own ears.

'Where—is—this?'

'You are in hospital.'

'I know that . . .'

'You have had an accident, Miss Forster. Please keep quite still—your leg and arm are in plaster.'

'Paul . . .' She closed her eyes again.

The nurse went to the door. After a whispered conversation, someone came into the room.

'Anna, you're with us again.'

It hurt even to look up at him. He knew this and said, 'Close them if you want to. I'll do the talking. You're going to be fine, darling, but you've needed rather a lot of sutures, so you will be very sore everywhere.'

'I—can't move and my head hurts—that too?'

'Some concussion. It could have been so much worse.'

She tried to lift her hand to feel her bandaged head, her face, under numerous dressings. 'Oh, no, no, no.'

'Anna—I'm here. Calm down. You need rest and quiet. They'll give you another shot and you can sleep. You're going to be all right, darling. Just try to relax. Your parents want to see you, just for a minute.'

'Oh, Paul, our holiday . . .' She didn't know that she was crying until the salt tears stung her face, seeping beneath the dressings.

'It's over now. You just have to get well—it may take a little time; but you're going to be fine.'

He lifted her hand to leave a kiss in the palm. She didn't remember anything else until she surfaced again next morning. Ralph and Eve had driven back to Reykjavik. It was just forty-eight hours since the accident and both Paul and her doctor at the hospital agreed that she could travel back to be near her parents at the City Hospital in Reykjavik without too much damage in their specially furnished ambulance.

'I shall be coming with you,' Paul said after he had given her the news, 'and will take full responsibility. But I think it will be easier all round if you're nearer to them.'

She recognised his hospital voice, the one he used to explain things to his patients, but it didn't properly register then, as she drifted in an abyss of pain in every part of her body.

Vaguely she heard him say to the nurse, 'She will need more sedation,' but she didn't know who they were talking about, nor did she care. It was all too much. She felt too weak and spiritless to fight.

In the ambulance, she lay watching the white, shiny roof, conscious of movement but not where they were taking her.

A nurse sat on the seat watching her, then, seeing her efforts, brought her a bowl. But it was Paul who held her through the waves of nausea; his hand supporting her head, which was opening and closing seemingly with every heart beat.

'We're almost there, now. Try to sleep again.' Paul's voice sounded far away. She heard herself groaning, but was powerless to stop.

Then, she was being wheeled along corridors with pale, gleaming walls. They hurt her eyes. She knew she was strapped to a stretcher; a nurse held her tubes and glucose bottle; Paul had gone.

She was in a small room, being lifted on to a plaster bed. Then, 'She's passed out again,' someone said. Then nothing.

There were voices in the room. A man's voice. A doctor. She knew he was a doctor. His voice was familiar. She had heard it before. Where? His fingers were cool on her wrist.

'It was moving her—but she seems more stable now. What a mess. She's certainly a lucky young woman.' Where had she heard it before? She opened her eyes but they were too heavy.

'How long will you leave those sutures in her face, Jön?' Paul's voice.

'Oh, five days, I think, or there may be scars. The deepest are on her legs, of course.'

Paul came to the bed. 'Are you awake, Anna? Open your eyes.'

Still heavy, she did as he asked.

'Hullo. How do you feel?'

'Awful.'

'Darling, Jön is taking care of you. You remember him at your parents' party?'

'Mmm . . .' She dare not move her head.

After that, faces came and went. Ralph, Eve, nurses, doctors. She slept, was wakened, slept again. Every slightest movement was pain. Stinging, burning, sharp, aching pain. She couldn't remember all that Paul had said about her injuries. But now she wanted to know. Dr Erikson seemed reluctant to summarise them when she asked. Her head, for one thing. Why was it bandaged?

'Are these straightforward fractures?' She was surprised at the strength of her own voice. So, obviously, was the nurse, covering a tray of instruments in one corner of the room. Her patient was indicating her plastered arm and tractioned leg. 'Can I see my notes?'

'You may not, Miss Forster,' Jön Erikson said, coming up to the bed. 'I'm very relieved to see you are so much better.'

'Why do I have a cage over this leg?'

'You have some fairly deep lacerations—and a number of sutures.'

'I am an S.R.N. in England, Dr Erikson. How many sutures? It seems rather extensive to me . . .'

'Eighteen.'

'Oh . . . And my face? Tell me . . .'

'They will soon heal. We shall be taking the sutures out in a few days.'

'I know. To reduce the—oh, I remember, the scars.' Against her will, tears welled up and spilled over. 'Am I going to be very marked?' she whispered through trembling lips. 'Am I?'

'It's too soon to know. You know that, don't you? Just leave it with us—it's early days.'

When her parents came that afternoon she was so depressed that their fears returned. Paul reassured them as much as he could.

'She has a hair-line skull fracture which will heal with rest quite soon, and stitches in the gash behind the ear. These will be removed in a week or so and the headaches will decrease. She needs lots of rest, but it will be a long time before she is over this, I'm afraid. We shall need a lot of patience too, knowing your daughter.'

Shocked, but relieved, they began to hope again.

'What about your own affairs, Paul? Your flight on Saturday? You have to go, don't you?'

'I shall wait until tomorrow, I think. Time to cancel then. She is in good hands—the best—and except for seeing her each day, there is very little else I can do.'

'And you do have commitments in Calderbury.'

'Also, a very important appointment on Wednesday. We'll see.'

'She won't want you to go.'

'I know,' he said slowly. 'There will probably be a changed behaviour pattern for a time, I think. But she's coming out of shock quite well. I hate leaving her like this. Anna has a lot to have to come to terms with. I'd like to help her do that. But you must. I'm sorry. Of course you will, you're her parents, but . . .' They saw his worried frown. Eve went out to the kitchen and plugged in for coffee, surreptitiously wiping her eyes so that the men wouldn't see her tears.

When she carried it in to them, Ralph was saying, 'We'll bring her home, Paul, the moment she is able to stand the journey.'

'Before too long, I hope. But I have yet to decide about tomorrow's flight.'

Ralph got up to answer the phone. Then he handed it to Paul. 'For you—someone called Bronwen?'

They saw him momentarily close his eyes before taking the receiver. 'Paul Keslar here.' Then, 'When was this, Bronwen?' and, after listening, 'Yes, of course. I shall be flying back tomorrow and will drive down from Heathrow.'

'So . . .' he told them, as he sank wearily down into one of the square chairs, 'it has been decided for me. My father has had a relapse—I have to go to him.'

His eyes were sad, his features haggard with too little sleep and his anxiety for Anna. Now this . . . He seemed to struggle for muscle control around his mouth. Eve thought there were tears in his eyes but she couldn't be sure.

After a time, he said that he would see Anna in the morning before he left and explain that he had no choice. 'I'm not sure how she will take it. If she was as normal as she usually is, there would be no question. But just now, she isn't thinking intro-spectively. She may think . . .'

'That you should be with her?' Eve put in.

'Something like that.' He didn't say what was in his mind. That she may think he was running away from her rather battered image; that Anna might not be able to live with her scarred face and limbs, or worse, think that he couldn't.

'You've both been marvellous. Thanks—for everything,' he told them now. 'We'll make up for it some time in the future. Plans have to be a little flexible, for a time, I'm afraid.'

'Your father?'

He nodded. 'Bronwen wouldn't get me home unless it was absolutely necessary. She is my father's nurse.'

Anna was a little more comfortable next morning. She even smiled when she saw Paul, looking at the clock beside her bed. 'So early?'

He explained why he must fly back as planned.

She heard him out without comment, but he saw her pupils darken and she looked sad.

'I hate to leave you, but your parents are going to bring you home as soon as you can travel. So get well soon. I'll be waiting.'

'Strange, isn't it?' She still slurred her words a little. 'Being on the receiving end. I didn't realise—how much one has to rely on one's nurse until now.'

He stood up.

'Must you go, so soon?'

'Yes.' He bent to kiss her mouth, where the dressings didn't quite meet, holding her hand between his. 'I love you . . . remember. Goodbye, my darling. Come home soon.'

Her hand slid away on to the bed cover.

'Goodbye,' she whispered, bravely, and not a tear escaped until he had closed the door after him.

Fortunately, her nurse came into the room before

they got too out of hand. She didn't cry again until the bandages were removed from her head and she felt the spiky new growth of her hair. Until then, she hadn't realised they had had to cut it very short. She hadn't known about the X-rays and suturing they'd had to do in those first hours after the accident.

'I want a mirror—please,' she begged her nurse, who postponed bringing her one.

Dr Jön, too, said that he would have one sent in for her. But it was her mother who recognised Anna's desperation and took her own from her handbag.

'It has been cut very short, dear, but it will soon grow again. We'll get it shampooed as soon as it's possible. It suits you—you look rather like an actress your father used to love—now what was her name? Caron, I think.'

'I look terrible . . .' Anna's voice sounded frozen. 'No wonder Paul couldn't wait to go.'

'He had no choice, Anna. He told you about his father.'

'He couldn't bear to look at me—I saw it in his eyes.'

'Don't cry, darling. Paul loves you very much, just the way you are. When you see him again, you will be just as . . .'

'Good as new?' She covered her facial dressings with both hands, grimacing because it hurt to talk.

'Dr Jön tells me they will take out those stitches tomorrow and the tightness will be less, not so painful.'

'That's usually my line. Why did this have to happen, just when I was so happy? I'm a nurse—I help people. Look, I'm just a mess. I'll always be a mess—I can't—even—move.'

'Calm down, Anna,' Dr Jön's voice cut in as he came into the room. 'Unless you want your headache to start up. Now—about those sutures.'

It was the authoritive voice she understood. It halted her rising hysteria as he meant it to.

She was missing Paul terribly. She missed the usual routine of her work at her own hospital and wondered why no-one had written to her. No-one cared. But no-one knew yet, Paul still being in Wales.

But one letter arrived from him and one from Gran, on the same day as it happened, and because the nurse opened it for her, she didn't see the Welsh postmark, imagining him to be at the Royal.

He missed her; hoped that she was beginning to cope better. Knowing her, she would find the de-termination needed to get on top of it—hoped the pain was less. He was very busy; the days not long enough. Rather a lot on my mind just now, darling, but you are never far from my thoughts, as you know. Come home soon. I need you.

Not one word about anyone at the Royal, she noticed. He's changed. I feel it. I'm no longer his lovely girl—I can sense the way he feels. It's me, my face, all of me. He knows I'll be scarred—I'm hideous . . . She touched her hair. Oh, just look at it—like a yellow hedgehog. Oh, God—he can't bear to look at me even. He doesn't even want me. How could he?

Her bitterness grew out of all proportion because she had too much time to brood about herself. I won't even be able to care for the patients, she thought. Who would want to look at me? And Paul's next letter did nothing to help matters. Because he didn't want to distress her further with the news that his father had died, he kept his letter short and, as Welsh people often are, it seemed a little abrupt to her sensitive mind, with clipped sentences which she interpreted wrongly.

'Oh, he's definitely cooled ...' she told herself. 'Perhaps next time may be the final one.' He had to think of his future and how could she become a consultant's wife, entertain his friends, when, 'Oh, no, no, no,' she sobbed into her pillow.

Don't worry, Paul, she decided. It's better if it comes from me. I know you won't want a scarred and possibly limping wife, because if her leg didn't mend properly, that's what she would be. Positively, no future—none that I can share with Paul. The dream was over.

She started her letter that night and asked her mother to post it next day. Eve had no idea what it contained. The first she knew was a phone call from Paul.

'She tells me that she has stopped loving me—has second thoughts about marriage altogether,' he said desperately. 'Hopes I will see things her way and accept her decision. Well, nothing in her present state is going to convince her otherwise, so we just wait; until you bring her home. She is suffering from a mutilation psychosis—most people who have had this kind of damage go through it in some form or another. We must just be very patient. Take care of her for me.'

'I am sure she hasn't changed towards you, Paul.'

'Well—she asks me to respect her feelings and not to write or try to see her.'

'Like you, I think this is psychosomatic.'

'I agree.'

'I'm so very sorry, Paul.'

'You'll keep me posted, won't you?'

'Of course.'

At the beginning of September, Anna came home. Though still on crutches and not yet out of plaster, her face was healing fast and Dr Jön thought the scars would barely show, especially with a little make-up. There was a long scar from thigh to knee which was taking a little longer to heal. Through her mother's vigilance and care her hair had regained its former silkiness and colour, but was still shorter than before. It didn't really matter. Nothing mattered to her now. She was in a state of apathy, lifting slightly, but the sparkle which was Annabel had gone. Her eyes were sad, her way of thinking had changed, her pleasure in the little things; and she hadn't even her work to look forward to because she couldn't go back to the Royal, with Paul there. Perhaps a hospital along the coast. Margate; later, when she was ready.

CHAPTER ELEVEN

BECAUSE Anna had heard nothing from Paul since Iceland, she believed that he had opted out gracefully. Yet now she found that difficult to relate to him; dropping a girl he professed to love, because she had an accident to her face. The other injuries didn't matter to her. But she had told him that she no longer loved him. Why should he not believe that and let her go?

Everyone in the village had been kind, dropping in with small presents; and one evening Jill Slade came with all the hospital news which only made things worse. Sister on Rowan had written a nice little letter to her and even Mr Lonsdale had sent a note and some flowers. But, because Jill hadn't known about Paul, she didn't think to mention him, until Anna asked.

'Oh, yes. He did go away for a couple of weeks somewhere, but he's back now. I heard a rumour, don't know if it's true, that he may be going to a hospital in Wales, as a consultant.'

'Oh . . .' Anna drew in her breath.

'Have you got a pain?'

She shook her head. No-one ever accepted the 'pain in the heart' theory, but she knew differently.

When Mervyn's landrover stopped at the gate at the weekend, as she sat in the garden, she turned and saw him crossing the lawn, looking bronzed, his hair bleached by the sun. Just as she remembered; his shirt sleeves were rolled to the elbows. He came quite naturally and sat down on the grass beside her. She loved him for not commenting on her changed appearance, except to ask,

'When are you getting rid of these things? The harvest supper is coming up, you know. Got to get some practice in before then.' He pushed her crutches nearer to her chair.

'I'm having the plaster off soon, then I can start some physiotherapy—after that . . .'

'You don't look any different. I thought you would. It was nasty by what I've heard. Had a rum old time of it, didn't you?' Not waiting for an answer he chattered on, 'I've seen you in the garden, but I didn't come sooner because we've been getting in the barley and oats. Good yield this year and the best apple crop ever.'

'I've heard the tractors going up and down the fields. I'm glad it's been a good year, Mervyn. You said I don't look any different. What about my hair, then?'

'Oh, that—a bit shorter, that's all. It'll soon grow. Besides, you used to wear it up sometimes. You are coming to the supper, aren't you? I'll come and fetch you.'

'No, not this year, but thanks, just the same, for asking me.'

He got up. 'Suit yourself, but I can come again, can't I? Cheer up—come chestnut time we'll be up in the woods gathering them in for Christmas and you'll be joining in. You'll see.'

He touched her shoulder in a kind of sympathetic gesture which made her throat ache a little. But she didn't often cry now.

Why couldn't she have fallen in love with someone like Mervyn? How simple it would all have been.

He accepted her as she was. She didn't feel any less a woman with him. How uncomplicated country people usually were. Always looking ahead, from one season to the next, planning the year. Next Sunday the church would be overflowing with vegetables and fruit and flowers. The same hymns of thanksgiving would be sung and meant, echoing out across the countryside. She envied them their basic faith.

It was a perfect September day. Eve and Gran wanted to go shopping in Calderbury, taking Anna's car. She watched them go, missing her car just then along with everything else. But next week her plaster was coming off. Not before time. It looked grubby now. Then, she supposed, weeks of physio—before she could think of tackling hospital duties again.

'Unthinkable—until after Christmas,' Sister had said the last time she was here.

'Three months. I'll go quietly mad,' Anna told Shane, in a seventh heaven as he lay panting beside her. But at least it was something to hang on to and, if Jill was right, Paul would no longer be at the Royal so there would be no danger of bumping into him. Only his memory.

Oh, Paul—you'll never know what it meant to let you go. I still need you so . . . But Jill had said he was away for two weeks. Had he gone to Wales then? Was that when his new post was finalised? She hoped his father need not know that they were no longer together. He had wanted his grandchildren to know and love that house too. She covered her face, recovering quickly when the car crunched on the gravel. They were back already.

It was Gran who announced innocently that they had met Paul in the town.

'He actually took us for coffee at that very expensive place near the car park. You know, where they have those gorgeous cream cakes.'

By the time she had finished, Anna had recovered sufficiently to say, 'He wasn't at the hospital then. Wednesday is outpatients clinic.'

'He was on his way to the bank, dear.' Eve was watching her carefully.

'How is he?'

'Much as usual. A little tired, perhaps. Over-worked probably. You knew his father had died.'

'No. When?'

'While we were in Iceland—he had to come back, don't you remember?'

'I thought . . .' She was silent.

'He told us that he has this new appointment at a hospital near his home in Wales. You know it, don't you? As a consultant, I believe,' Gran said calmly. 'I knew he had the makings of one but it's rather soon, isn't it? We wished him well . . .'

'I suppose,' Eve put in, 'this opportunity just came up and he was right for it. Now, what about lunch? Shall we have it out here?'

Anna spent the whole afternoon thinking hard about Paul. She couldn't not think once she knew all the facts. It might begin to get better, when he was no longer around. She wondered if he would live in the house and what would happen to Bronwen. Mrs Hughes would no doubt stay as she had nowhere else. It was her home too.

She couldn't concentrate on the magazines her mother had brought her, gazing instead at the tall clumps of purple michaelmas daisies and the colour-ful borders of dahlias, a riot of red and orange this year. She supposed she was lucky to be able to lie there and just look. But oh, I would give anything to be back on Rowan, she thought. It's the only panacea for the emptiness I feel.

A car turned quietly into the driveway behind her own. Even Shane's bark of welcome didn't warn her, until she turned to see who had come visiting. By that time, Paul was out and coming with the positive strides she remembered across the lawn. There was no way she could prevent it, even if she had wanted to. He came on—purposefully.

Then, he took her face in his hands and kissed her gently. Ignoring the scars, he wiped the tears away with one of her tissues, as they ran down her cheeks.

'These, my darling, are the last tears you are going to shed, for a very long time. Why did you send me away?'

'Oh, Paul—I thought you couldn't bear to look at me, the way I was—even now. I thought I was letting you out. You see—as I saw it, when I needed you most, you just went away.'

'Bronwen sent for me. I couldn't tell you—my father died two days after I got there.'

'I'm so sorry. I only heard today. If I had known, I would have understood.'

'I'm not sure that you would, my darling. You were looking for a way out at that time. It didn't matter, how you looked. I know what you are. Don't you think I was just as shattered as you were? You just don't stop loving someone because they've been hurt. Because their image has changed for a while. It was yourself you were out of love with, wasn't it?'

'Yes—I know that now. But Gran says that you are going to live in Wales—that you're a consultant now. Congratulations. I'm so glad about that, Paul.'

'I take it up in the New Year. But you're going to marry me before then, aren't you, Anna?'

'You really want that?'

'More than ever. It's been a long waiting time. Nothing has changed; except that these things get in the way and I can't be close enough to you.'

'Next week.'

'Too long. What about coming in tomorrow?'

Then he was drawing her into his arms, holding her so that she needed no crutch for support, lifting her face until he only had to bend his to touch her lips, the way she remembered.

Gran, coming out into the garden, saw him kissing the back of her neck, twisting a strand of hair in his finger; she raised her eyebrows and quickly went in again.

Paul was saying delightedly, 'Your golden curl is back again—I think your hair will be just the right length for our wedding.'

'Oh, Paul, only you can make me feel so good again. I wanted to be perfect for you, and now . . .'

'I didn't say I wanted a perfect wife, Anna, just the lovely girl I know you to be,' and against her ear, 'Mrs Forster Senior is hovering in the porch. Shall we go and tell them—or do you think she knows already?'

'Dear Gran . . .' Anna said, picking up her crutch and keeping in step with Paul as they went towards the house. 'She was in at the beginning, wasn't she?'

'So she tells me.'

'She's happy because my parents are coming back here, permanently. Dad has decided that enough is enough and is definitely retiring at Christmas. I shall miss this part of the world,' she said nostalgically, as they stopped to look across at the orchards, dripping with rosy colour still.

'You'll be back. As often as you like. Imagine how the children will enjoy those woods. We must go down soon to see what changes you want made; new curtains and decor. I want you to do just as you like there. It's going to be your home too, you know now. You must love it too . . .'

'I do already,' she said, throwing down her crutch and taking his arm instead as they went into the house.

Two more
Doctor Nurse Romances
to look out for this month

Mills & Boon Doctor Nurse Romances are proving
very popular indeed. Stories range wide throughout
the world of medicine – from high-technology
modern hospitals to the lonely life of a nurse in a
small rural community.
These are the other two titles for November.

A BRIDE FOR THE SURGEON
by Hazel Fielding
By marrying Pip, Hallam Fielding would gain a clinic nurse, a
general secretary, cook, housekeeper and slave – and all for free!
Even if he could never love her, was if sufficient if she could
somehow make him want her?

NURSE RHONA'S ROMANCE
by Anne Vinton
Rhona was disappointed, though not heartbroken, when her
romance with Chris Willson came to nothing: all the same, she
was glad to have her work as a district nurse to take her mind
off things. And she was even more thankful for her career when
her next romance, with Dr Alex Denham, crashed to disaster.

On sale where you buy Mills & Boon romances

The Mills & Boon rose is the rose of romance

How to join in a whole new world of romance

It's very easy to subscribe to the Mills & Boon Reader Service. As a regular reader, you can enjoy a whole range of special benefits. Bargain offers. Big cash savings. Your own free Reader Service newsletter, packed with knitting patterns, recipes, competitions, and exclusive book offers.

We send you the very latest titles each month, postage and packing free – no hidden extra charges. There's absolutely no commitment – you receive books for only as long as you want.

We'll send you details. Simply send the coupon – or drop us a line for details about the Mills & Boon Reader Service Subscription Scheme.
Post to: Mills & Boon Reader Service, P.O. Box 236, Thornton Road, Croydon, Surrey CR9 3RU, England.
*Please note: READERS IN SOUTH AFRICA please write to: Mills & Boon Ltd., P.O. Box 1872, Johannesburg 2000, S. Africa.

Please send me details of the Mills & Boon Subscription Scheme.

NAME (Mrs/Miss) _____ EP3

ADDRESS _____

_____

COUNTY/COUNTRY_____ POST/ZIP CODE_____
BLOCK LETTERS, PLEASE

Mills & Boon
the rose of romance